From The Wo...
34 Great Sutton S...

Suniti Namjoshi was born in India in 1941. She has worked as an Officer in the Indian Administrative Service and in academic posts in India and Canada. Since 1972 she has taught in the Department of English of the University of Toronto and now lives in Devon.

She has published numerous poems, fables, articles and reviews in anthologies, collections and literary and Women's Studies journals in India, Canada, the U.S. and Britain. She has published five books of poetry in India and two in Canada, *The Authentic Lie*, 1982, and *From the Bedside Book of Nightmares*, 1984. Her first book of fiction, *Feminist Fables*, was published by Sheba Feminist Publishers in 1981; her second, *The Conversations of Cow*, by the Women's Press in 1985; her third, *Aditi and the one-eyed monkey*, written for children, by Sheba Feminist Publishers in 1986; and her fourth, *The Blue Donkey Fables*, by The Women's Press in 1988. With Gillian Hanscombe she has written the sequence of poems *Flesh and Paper*, published in 1986 by Ragweed in Canada and in both book and audio cassette form by Jezebel Tapes and Books in Britain.

SUNITI NAMJOSHI

The Mothers
of Maya Diip

The Women's Press

Published by The Women's Press Limited 1989
A Member of the Namara Group
34 Great Sutton Street, London EC1V 0DX

Copyright © Suniti Namjoshi 1989
All rights reserved

British Library Cataloguing in Publication Data
Namjoshi, Suniti, 1941–
  The mothers of Maya Diip.
  I. Title
  823 [F]

ISBN 0–7043–4200–6

Phototypeset by Input Typesetting Ltd
Printed in Great Britain by
BPCC Hazell Books Ltd
Member of BPCC Ltd
Aylesbury, Bucks, England

*For Ai, my grandmother,
the late Laxmi Devi Naik Nimbalkar*

'Let Looking Glass creatures, whatever they be,
Come and dine with the Red Queen, the White Queen,
and me!'

Contents

PART I

1. A proper matriarchy — 5
2. The Maternal Spirit — 9
3. Being a Mayan — 16
4. Children are wonderful — 26
5. An ordinary woman — 32
6. A little preview — 41
7. Well, Poet? — 49
8. Day of Oracles — 55

PART II

9. Being Eater or Eaten — 63
10. But she was a heretic — 69
11. A loyal Mayan — 75
12. Ashan babies — 82
13. Loathsome reptile — 89
14. It's a privilege — 98
15. The helicopter shuddered — 105

PART III

16. Will you have us? — 113
17. The poetic thing — 120
18. What's your part? — 127
19. Write a poem — 135
20. Is that what you mean? — 141

Acknowledgments

My thanks to the Canada Council for financial assistance; to Christine Donald, Sue Gilbert and Jackie Pearson for their comments; and to Gill Hanscombe, in particular, for her patience and help with the final revision.

PART I

'But what would you do if you were the Red Queen?'
'I would make everybody behave themselves,' Alice said firmly.
'How?'
'Well,' began Alice –

1

A proper matriarchy

Of all the princely states of India there was one in which a matriarchy bloomed unashamedly. Perhaps it was the soil, perhaps the climate, perhaps it was the location and the fortuitous accidents of genetic history. Perhaps it was the goddess (whom feminists in the west beseech intermittently). Or perhaps it was the happy line of competent queens.

Whatever the cause, when the Blue Donkey received a formal invitation from the Ranisaheb to visit the principality, she felt highly gratified and then dubious. Was this a joke or had she been recognised? There were rumours about that a matriarchy did exist, but no one was quite sure whether it was historical fact, a legend or a dream. The thought that it might be a functioning reality made feminists tremble. They spoke in hushed voices and exchanged scraps of paper which they told one another were mutilated messages from the Maternal Deep. When it was discovered that some of the feminists had been circulating their own work cleverly disguised as oracular tit-bits, the uncertainty and the excitement multiplied.

The Blue Donkey kept quiet about her invitation. She only told her friend, Jyanvi. After all, Jyanvi was an Indian and a feminist; she was also a poet, she might take it seriously.

Jyanvi was nice about it. 'Well done,' she said. 'Where exactly are the Maternal Deeps?'

The Blue Donkey frowned. 'Off the west coast of India. Surely you've heard of the Ma' Deep?'

'Oh. You mean Maya Diip, don't you? "Diip" means a lamp, not a deep or a dip. And "dwip" means an island or place of refuge. Yes, I've heard of it.'

'And what does "Maya" mean?' asked the Blue Donkey crossly.

'Compassionate or illusory.'

'Well, which is it?'

'I don't know.'

'Don't you want to know?'

'I suppose so.'

'Well, then accompany me. It says here I can bring a friend provided she is adult and civilised.'

Jyanvi lowered her eyes modestly. 'What are we going to do once we get there?'

'Recite poetry.'

'Be serious.'

'That's what it says here. The inhabitants of Maya actually like it.'

'Who has invited you?'

'The Queen.'

'Are they allowed to have queens?'

'What do you mean?'

'I mean, if it's a proper matriarchy – '

'There have to be matriarchs,' the Blue Donkey finished for her. 'Look, it says right here, "Ranisaheb", and even I know that that means Queen. It does not mean the Feminist Poetry Collective.'

'In that case ought we to go?'

'Yes,' said the Blue Donkey unhesitatingly.

At Bombay airport they were met by Saraswati. She greeted them with her hands joined together and introduced herself. Jyanvi fell in love instantly.

'What does "Saraswati" mean?' asked the Blue Donkey.

'Saraswati is a goddess,' Jyanvi whispered back.

The Blue Donkey snorted, but said nothing.

They were taken to a yacht. Once they were all comfortably settled, Saraswati smiled. It was brilliant October, gulls flew about, the waves were playful. 'Arms, legs and limbs/ the curve of your throat/ when the goddess made you . . . Shut up,' Jyanvi told herself fiercely. 'These are unpolished lines, and their standards are probably high.' She tried to look capable of the wry rejoinder, the witty aside, the lifted eyebrow and the deprecating smile. She was ready.

'And how are your children?' Saraswati asked.

Jyanvi blinked, but the Blue Donkey took it in her stride. 'In my youth,' she informed Saraswati kindly, 'I took a vow of celibacy. I have eschewed sex.'

'What has that to do with children?'

'Ummm. I see your point. The fact is,' the Blue Donkey went on cautiously, 'neither Jyanvi nor I have any children.'

'At least she didn't say I dislike the little beasts,' Jyanvi thought. She felt uneasy.

'But what is your rank?' Saraswati had been startled into asking outright. She apologised. 'I beg your pardon, but if neither of you has attained motherhood, then how did you achieve adult status?'

The Blue Donkey glanced at Jyanvi, but Jyanvi was staring hard at the sea.

'Are all the adults on Maya Diip mothers?' asked the Blue Donkey carefully.

'Of course.' Saraswati looked puzzled. 'Ah. I take your point. You must have thought I meant Grade A status. You must forgive me. I have rushed in foolishly and trampled on griefs which of their nature must take a long time to heal. I meant no harm.' She put her arm around Jyanvi, half in supplication, half in affection. Jyanvi could smell the flowers in her hair, the sandalwood on her skin. 'Please,' she heard Saraswati say, 'please, do say it's quite all right.'

'It's – it's quite all right,' mumbled Jyanvi. She rallied. 'And how are your children?' she asked politely.

Saraswati beamed. 'So far I have only been permitted one

daughter. Her name is Sona. By the grace of the goddess she has done well in the tests and is thought to be promising.'

The Blue Donkey decided they had better find out more before they asked further questions. 'The goddess is kind,' she murmured. 'We are tired after our long journey and would like to rest.'

2

The Maternal Spirit

In the palace Gagri the Good was on the rampage again. She had kicked and screamed, had been hauled away to an upper room and had howled unceasingly for more than an hour. Everyone had a slight headache, except the Ranisaheb, who went on munching a plateful of pakoras, receiving visitors, granting some favours, refusing others, dispensing justice and acceding to a few unmade requests. What made the Matriarch so hard to handle was the incalculability of the basis of her judgment. Some attributed this to her extreme intelligence, wit and knowledge. Others saw it as a political ploy, a means of suggesting that the ways of the Matriarch were quite as mysterious as those of the goddess. The Five Great Families were getting tired of it, but there was little that the Lesser Matriarchs could do. By a judicious use of the permissions and prohibitions licensing motherhood she had manipulated the web of kinship patterns so that in the end the flow of loyalties all led to her. She was a Grade A mother three times over (that was the maximum), she herself was the product of a Grade A mother three times over, she had magnificent teeth, an excellent appetite, she was always clad in green, and she always prevailed, or, at least, she frequently did.

Her present visitor was her friend, the Lesser Matriarch,

Malini Devi. She was tall and thin, fair for a Mayan. She adjusted the folds of her grey sari.

'Tell me,' she began, 'if a friend betrays a friend, are debts and obligations immediately cancelled?'

The Ranisaheb smiled. She knew that Malini Devi was furious with her. Why couldn't the woman accept that, in this instance, she would not bend the rules? It would be stupid.

'No.' She answered Malini Devi in her grandest manner. 'No, the vows of friendship are eternal and not to be shaken by small disagreements over minor matters.'

'This can hardly be called a minor matter!' Malini Devi expostulated. Then she altered her tone. 'Will you not grant my niece Grade B status?' She disliked pleading, but was willing to do it this once.

'Malini, I will not change the laws of the state. Sarla Devi already has Grade A status with the proviso that she may not be a biological mother. If she's desperate to have the bar removed, then clearly she must resign her office.'

'But that isn't fair! Why should she have to resign?'

'You know why as well as anyone. Ever since the feud between the Third Matriarch and the Chief of the Temple the law has been in force. The Chief of the Goddess' Guild may not bear a daughter, and no daughter of the Mayan Matriarch may enter the Guild. Come, don't presume on our friendship.'

'But she needs to have a child.'

The Ranisaheb began to lose patience. 'Then let her have a boy!'

Malini Devi flinched under the contempt in the Matriarch's voice. 'No!' she cried out.

The Matriarch sighed. 'Malini, why does it matter so much? My daughter, Shyamila, has already pleaded with me on Sarla's behalf. After all, when Shyamila bears a daughter, Sarla Devi will be her co-mother. Then she'll have a child.'

Malini Devi shook her head. 'You know very well it's not the same thing.'

The Matriarch shrugged. 'Why not? I gave you Saraswati, my own daughter, to adopt. You've said yourself that you couldn't have loved her more had she been your own flesh and blood. What's more, Saraswati has a daughter who promises well. Your house won't die.'

Malini Devi clutched the edge of the Ranisaheb's sari. 'But don't you see? I have no children of my own. And if my niece has no child, my bloodline will die!'

The Ranisaheb turned away. 'All children are the gift of the goddess.' It was a dismissal. Malini Devi was to understand that the platitude was her final word on that particular subject.

Anger and frustration drove the Lesser Matriarch to her feet. 'You have an heir!'

Just then Gagri the Good rushed into the room. She paused when she saw the Lesser Matriarch. Malini Devi ignored the child. With a perfunctory gesture, she turned on her heel. She began to walk away. The Ranisaheb summoned her back.

'Sit down. You haven't been given permission to leave. Now, why should it trouble you that I have an heir? You have one too.'

'It's not the same thing. You want to make sure that if Shyamila and Sarla ally themselves, the children of that alliance will be your granddaughters.'

The Matriarch laughed. 'Don't be absurd. Why should I care?'

'Because you want the next Matriarch to be of your descent.'

'I, who exiled my own daughter?'

'You had no choice. Your daughter, Asha, blasphemed against Maya itself.'

Gagri the Good listened avidly. They were talking about the Forbidden Subject. But then the grown-ups glanced at her and nothing more was said.

The Ranisaheb regarded the Lesser Matriarch with cold disdain. 'You forget yourself. You also forget who I am. You may leave now.'

Malini Devi realised that she had gone too far. 'Please,' she tried to excuse herself. 'I didn't mean to make you angry. You don't know what it is to be childless.'

The Matriarch remained unmoved. 'Isn't Saraswati your daughter?' she enquired icily.

Malini Devi could not keep the bitterness out of her voice. 'Yes,' she retorted. 'But she's also yours!' With that she left.

Gagri the Good snuggled up to her grandmother and burrowed into the folds of her sari. She liked the feel of the fine cotton. Her grandmother always smelled of mogra flowers. Gagri felt safe and warm. She had forgotten about her mother. She began to play with the glass green bangles and the gold ones on her grandmother's wrist.

'You're a little darling, aren't you?' the Matriarch murmured.

Gagri the Good wriggled happily. 'Yes,' she said.

Then she ran away to climb the drainpipes. Two Grade C mothers followed quickly. Five minutes later the howling and screaming began again. She had fallen into a fishpond while jumping across it and one of the Grade C mothers had immediately insisted that she get changed. Her grandmother liked to see her impeccably dressed. She usually wore the loose blouses and skirts appropriate to little girls; and since these frequently got torn, at least one Grade C mother was kept in employment.

'Amuse me.' The Matriarch smiled at her daughters.

Dinner was over. The Blue Donkey had been particularly pleased by the saffron rice and by the fact that the food had been vegetarian. The Matriarch had presided, her enormous bulk clad, as usual, in a green sari. It was evident that she had enjoyed both the food and the company. She had made a genial host, but in spite of that the Blue Donkey wondered if the others were a little afraid of her, all of them except Gagri the Good, who, by virtue of her age, was somehow exempt. The servants had cleared the table, and Jyanvi and the Blue Donkey were now sitting in the drawing room with the others. They had been settled in the palace and introduced to Valerie, who, they were told, was a western immigrant. Jyanvi had hoped that Saraswati would stay, but she had said that she was a Grade A mother and must tend to her daughter; she would try to return later. They had also been introduced to the Matriarch's daughters, Shyamila the Civil and Pramila the Poet. Gagri the Good had been sent to bed after half an hour of bribes and promises, and

Saraswati had returned after putting her own daughter to bed. The Matriarch glanced at her fondly. There were times when the Matriarch wished that she had kept Saraswati and packed off Pramila the Poet instead. From the corner of her eye she saw Pramila getting ready to recite. 'Guests first,' she said sharply. Pramila subsided.

Valerie rose. 'Your Highness,' she announced, 'I have written a poem in your honour:

> Here by the grace of the Mayan Queen
> I can be at last who I've always been.'

'A good couplet,' responded the Matriarch. 'But who is it whom you've always been and why are you able to be her now?'

'Because, Your Highness, now at last I'm a woman amongst women.' Valerie looked so moved and upset by her own lines that it would have been a cruelty to question her further.

Shyamila the Civil smiled at Jyanvi. 'Your turn now.'

Jyanvi gulped. She hadn't realised she'd be expected to improvise, but Saraswati was looking at her – Saraswati the Beautiful, more elegant than ever in pale printed silk. Jyanvi gulped again and blurted out briefly,

> 'Children may howl and children may squall.
> The Maternal Spirit rides over all.'

'Not bad,' murmured Pramila, 'but may I suggest that you delete the "and" in the first line, and somehow reduce the syllables in the second? Perhaps "overrides" would be better than "rides over"? There's an extra stress . . . Or better still just a verb which needs no preposition. How's this?

> Children may howl, children may squall.
> The Maternal Spirit embraces all.'

'It's a different poem,' protested the Blue Donkey.

'Ah, yes, so it is.' She looked around the room owlishly.

The light glinted off her spectacles. Jyanvi thought she looked pathetic. She was so anxious to please, to gain her mother's approval . . . Even her sari did not hide her angularities. Jyanvi glanced down at her own jeans. Valerie in her sarong was better dressed than she was. She felt scruffy. But the Ranisaheb was nodding to Saraswati.

Saraswati threw Jyanvi a mischievous glance. She said,

> 'Two strangers came to our shore.
> They asked one question and asked no more.'

'And what was the question they did ask?' demanded the Matriarch.

'Whether all the adults on Maya were mothers.'

The Matriarch seemed amused, but Shyamila the Civil said courteously, 'We know that in the patriarchies, matters are different. Do not be embarrassed. Ask what you wish. We will try to answer.'

Jyanvi felt reckless. 'Why are children glorified here? Don't the lives and longings of women matter?' She risked a glance at Saraswati; Saraswati appeared unoffended.

It was Valerie who was protesting, 'Oh no, it's not like that at all. As you know, in the patriarchies, the children govern; and though to be a woman is bad, to be a mother is usually worse. Here on Maya we have the Rule of the Mothers, and the Rule of the Mothers is just, gentle and generous.'

The Matriarch smiled, Pramila muttered that the alliteration was perhaps just a little overdone, and Shyamila, seeing that Jyanvi and the Blue Donkey looked puzzled, said to them, 'I will tell you a story. There was once a child who did not wish to grow up. She played with the pretty boys all day long. Her dolls gathered dust. She fished and swam and climbed tall trees. She explained to her mothers, "You have made a mistake. I should have been a boy. Look how I run and dazzle and dance in the sun." Mother A said, "You are a foolish child. The goddess has graced you. Some day you will grow into your full womanhood and you will embrace the sea and the air and the goddess herself and your daughters to come in your strong arms; and then you will be a woman among women." And Mother B said, "I prayed for a daughter, and when you were cradled in my belly I fed and sustained you so that your bones would knit well and my line carry on." And the C mothers said, "We clothed you and cleaned you, we taught you and trained you. Was it all for nothing? There must come a day when you gather about you the robes of womanhood and we know that our work was well done." But the little girl stamped her foot. "I do not want to be a mother," she told all her mothers. "It's a thankless task and a lot of work. Being a child is much more fun." Mother A groaned, Mother B moaned and all the C mothers winced and frowned. It was no use. The little girl refused to become a womanly woman. The years went by. She did no lessons, she failed her tests, the boys she had played with dived into the sea and turned into foam; but she continued eternally young. And then one day she turned fifteen. Her mothers informed her that for better or for worse their work was done. Suddenly she discovered that though still a child, she belonged to no one.'

'What happened to her?' Jyanvi had been listening to the tale intently.

'Nothing happened. If you see an elderly woman walking the streets who begs to be mothered – why, that's her.' Shyamila shrugged. 'A pitiful spectacle.'

The story had been told for the benefit of the guests, but neither Jyanvi nor the Blue Donkey had much to say. Soon the company retired. Valerie, trying to be helpful, had pointed the moral: 'This society has no use at all for childish women.' It perturbed Jyanvi, and then she was cross with herself for being perturbed. That there had been extra warmth in Saraswati's manner when she said good night made matters worse. She slept badly that night and dreamed that she and Saraswati had married each other. In the dream they had entered a great house, but they could not lie down; it was crammed with children.

3

Being a Mayan

In the palace garden Valerie was sounding out the Blue Donkey, trying to arrive at her political affiliations, her views on life, and which side she was likely to choose on the Question of the Succession. The Blue Donkey was being agreeable. She liked gardens, and these were extensive. Because of the monsoon everything was cool and green. It had rained earlier that morning, but the sun was out now and she could feel its warmth on her back. She looked up at the blazing blue sky and then looked around her at the great banyans, the tamarinds and the neem trees, at the small mogra bushes and the variety of crotons. The air was gentle and felt benign.

'How do you like it here?' began Valerie.

'It's very pleasant.' The Blue Donkey was not to be drawn. She needed to get her bearings first.

'And what do you think of our Matriarch?' Valerie continued.

'A formidable figure.'

'Now that you're here, do you think you'll stay?'

'Surely that depends,' murmured the Blue Donkey. She nibbled a blade of grass.

'On what?' Valerie was persistent.

'On whether we're asked.'

'I'm sure you'll be asked. The Matriarch likes you. I've lived here for the past ten years.'

The Blue Donkey decided that it was her turn to ask questions. 'It seems then that the Ranisaheb is an absolute monarch. Is that so?'

'Oh no.' Valerie realised that the Blue Donkey didn't, after all, know very much. 'She's only the head of the Mayan Council. The other members are the Five Lesser Matriarchs, but she can always outwit them. Besides, they're all related to each other.'

The Blue Donkey took this in. 'But isn't the Council answerable to anyone?' she wanted to know.

'Oh yes,' Valerie replied. 'The Council is responsible to the Chiefs of the Guilds.'

'Guilds?'

'Yes. The Guild of Poets, the Guild of Builders, the Guild of Servants, the Guild of Mathematicians and so forth. You see, all Grade C mothers are members of a Guild'.

'What about Grade B mothers?' the Blue Donkey asked.

'Oh, they're biological mothers,' Valerie told her. 'It's just a description. Usually all Grade A mothers are automatically given Grade B status.'

'I don't quite follow,' said the Blue Donkey politely. She felt hopelessly muddled.

Valerie smiled indulgently. She remembered for an instant how confusing it had been for her when she first came to Maya. 'Well,' she explained, 'Grade A mothers are the chosen few. They pass all the tests and go on to become the Chiefs of Guilds and so on. Their main privilege is that they're expected to have daughters right away. They usually bear their own daughters, but not always. Take Sarla Devi, for instance. She's a Grade A mother, but isn't allowed to bear her own daughter because she's the Chief of the Guild of the Goddess' Servants.'

Valerie paused when she noticed that the Blue Donkey was looking more puzzled than ever. 'Shall I stop?' she asked.

'No, no. Please carry on,' the Blue Donkey murmured hastily.

Valerie carried on. 'Now Grade B mothers, as I explained, just means biological mothers. And Grade C mothers do the work. When they've worked long enough and can pay to have a daughter, then they can apply for Grade A status. The main thing is that all mothers are members of Guilds. Except, of course, the Matriarch.'

The Blue Donkey nodded. It still seemed very complicated. 'I think I understand,' she said to Valerie. 'But tell me, where do Blue Donkeys fit in?'

'Why, for the time being at least, you're an honoured guest. But you must find a Matron if you plan to stay on.'

'What is a Matron?' asked the Blue Donkey.

Valerie sighed. There was so much to explain. But in a way she was enjoying her role as native guide to this benighted foreigner. 'A Matron is just a person, usually a matriarch,' she replied. 'If you are her client, you look to her for help and support.'

'And in return?'

'In return you owe her your allegiance.'

'It sounds like a racket,' muttered the Blue Donkey and kicked absent-mindedly at a pebble.

'Oh no,' Valerie protested. 'It's almost maternal. And, rightly perceived, it does honour to both.'

'Have you a Matron?'

'Oh yes. It's generally known that I am under the protection of Pramila the Poet.'

'Is she a matriarch?'

'Well, no. But she is a princess. Besides, she's also the Chief of the Guild of Poets. If you like I could put in a word for you . . .'

Up to this point they had been strolling along, but the thought of Pramila the Poet as her Matron made the Blue Donkey come to a halt. 'Oh,' she said, 'that is most kind, but I'm still very confused and need time . . .'

Valerie let the subject drop. They entered a coconut grove and almost immediately saw Gagri the Good up a coconut palm, trying to shake loose a few coconuts.

'Isn't that dangerous?' enquired the Blue Donkey.

'No, it's all right. Look, there are two Grade C mothers holding a net under her.'

The Blue Donkey looked at the women. 'Surely two grown-up women have better things to do?'

'Under the Rule of the Mothers,' Valerie murmured, 'children prosper, especially if the child is the Matriarch's granddaughter.'

'But which one of her daughters is Gagri's mother?' asked the Blue Donkey. 'Is it Shyamila? They didn't behave like mother and daughter – I mean, except in so far as all women are mothers, of course,' she added quickly.

'Oh no, Shyamila and Pramila have no daughters yet. Gagri's mother's name was Asha. She was the Matriarch's eldest daughter.'

'What happened to her? Is she dead?'

'Not exactly.' Valerie hesitated. 'She was debarred from the succession and sent into exile.'

'What for?'

'For being a heretic.'

'What did she say?'

'She said that the pretty boys deserved better.' Valerie blurted this out quickly. 'Look,' she went on, 'the Apostasy of Asha is not a subject that a good Mayan should ever discuss. Let's talk about something else.'

'All right,' the Blue Donkey agreed. She could see that Valerie was upset. They walked back slowly. After a while the Blue Donkey asked, 'Who is likely to be the Matriarch's Successor?'

Valerie shrugged. 'It's a vexed question, and if it isn't settled soon, may cause trouble. The Matriarch's getting on. She herself favours Gagri the Good, but the child is only eight.'

'Does the Matriarch's Successor have to be her daughter or her granddaughter?'

'In theory, no. In theory all the Daughters of Maya look to the Matriarch as an incarnation of the Supreme Mother; but in practice the bloodline has been unbroken for seven hundred years.'

As they approached the palace the Blue Donkey asked, 'And who controls the army?'

'We have no army, just the Therapists' Guild. They're the police. They deal chiefly with crimes of passion.'

'Passion?'

'Yes. Maladjusted mothers, unsisterly sisters, rivalries and jealousies of diverse sorts, non-conformity with Mayan customs, and, of course,' she nodded in the direction of Saraswati and Jyanvi who appeared to be having a heated discussion in the middle of the courtyard, 'the problems of lovers.' They saw Jyanvi break off angrily and hurry back to the palace. Saraswati followed at leisure.

'And who controls the police?'

'Shyamila the Civil. They're all trained in therapy, you know. She is the Chief of the Guild of Therapists.'

'Is that the most powerful Guild?' the Blue Donkey enquired.

Valerie considered. 'Yes,' she replied, 'that and the Guild of the Goddess' Servants. She paused and added, 'Shyamila's lover, Sarla Devi, is the Chief of that.' She looked at the Blue Donkey.

The Blue Donkey realised that it was a significant remark, but she didn't know how to respond. 'It's a complex society,' she ventured at last.

Valerie grinned. 'That it is. No individual isolated and each woman bound to the others by ties of kinship, accepted loyalties and professional affiliations.'

'I can see why one would need a Matron here,' the Blue Donkey muttered. 'Why didn't you choose the Matriarch herself?'

Valerie shrugged. 'One has to be chosen. I made the mistake of reprimanding Gagri a few years ago.'

'What happened?'

'The child was making a nuisance of herself. I said something.'

'And then?'

'Then I fell out of favour.'

The Blue Donkey stared at a bed of marigolds. She didn't quite know how to phrase her next question. At last she said, 'Don't you find this kowtowing and currying for favour a bit difficult?'

Valerie shrugged. 'I was married and divorced before I came here. Coping with the mothers of Maya isn't all that hard. At least they think they ought to behave like responsible adults.'

She lowered her voice. 'You see, it's all a matter of figuring out how things work.'

'Being a Mayan isn't easy, is it?' said the Blue Donkey gently. 'Thank you for explaining these difficult matters.'

Valerie laughed. 'Oh, you'll soon get the hang of it. See you at the Festival.' She turned back to add, 'By the way, your friend, Jyanvi, is aiming pretty high. Saraswati belongs to the Five Great Families. The Matriarch is her biological mother. And, next to Gagri, it's generally believed that the Matriarch favours her.'

The Blue Donkey looked at Jyanvi sideways. They had told Valerie they would find their way to the Festival Pavilion. Cows jostled them, children ran about, there were a few bicycles, an occasional car, and, of course, women, grown-up women, the mothers of Maya, eddying past. The Blue Donkey was worried. At last she said, 'What were you and Saraswati arguing about in the garden this morning?'

'I told her I was in love with her,' Jyanvi mumbled.

'What did she say?'

'She said that she would carefully consider my application to be one of her lovers. I think she was teasing me.'

'I see.' The Blue Donkey looked at Jyanvi quizzically. 'What did you say?'

'Well,' Jyanvi sounded embarrassed, 'I got angry. I said I didn't want to be just one of her lovers, I was serious.'

'And she?'

'She asked me what I meant — was I asking to take on the co-mothership of her daughter, Sona? I couldn't see what that had to do with anything, but I asked what it involved. And she said it meant joint responsibility for the raising of the child.'

The Blue Donkey felt sorry for Jyanvi. 'And then?' she probed gently.

'I asked how old Sona was. And she said that that was irrelevant.'

'And then?'

'Then we seemed on the verge of quarrelling, so I walked away.'

'That was a bit rude.'

'Well, I couldn't very well say I wasn't interested in her child, only in her, could I?'

Jyanvi had raised her voice. The Blue Donkey shot her a warning glance. After a pause she said quietly, 'Jyanvi, do you realise who you've been dealing with?'

'Who?'

'Very possibly the Matriarch's Successor.'

'I don't care,' muttered Jyanvi. She sounded miserable.

They walked on in silence. As they drew near the Festival Pavilion the Blue Donkey cautioned, 'You're reciting this evening. Be careful.' But she got no response. Jyanvi appeared not to have heard her.

They entered the great hall. Someone put a garland around Jyanvi's neck and pushed her towards the platform. The Blue Donkey made her way through the crowd and settled down near Saraswati. On stage there were two other poets besides Jyanvi, and behind them a group of musicians: one was a tabalji, another had a veena, and the third a tamboura. The tabla sounded. Pramila the Poet made her way to the centre of the platform. She was splendidly dressed in a brocaded sari of heavy silk. Emerald earrings studded her ears. 'Borrowed from the Matriarch,' Saraswati whispered. The clothes of the other women were more modest. Jyanvi had exchanged her jeans for a cotton sarong and an embroidered shirt. She looked as though she almost belonged, but something about her was not quite Mayan. The hall was almost full now. In spite of the open windows, the smell of the perfumed coconut oil from the women's hair hung like a cloud. It was giving Jyanvi a headache. She looked dazed, a little nervous.

'May the goddess smile upon us!' Pramila cried out.

'May the goddess rejoice!' the audience returned.

Pramila introduced the poets. 'I will recite the first poem.' She smiled archly. 'That will set the mood, the tone, and the theme for the contest. It will remain for each of these poets to improvise a piece that fits in with the first.' She cleared her throat.

> The Song of the Grade A Mother
>
> First I worked hard,
> Then I worked harder,
> Then my daughters came.
>
> They sang and they yelped.
> My sisters all helped.
> Life was never the same.
>
> Now my daughters are mothers.
> They look to the others.
> They are gentle and just and sane.

The audience clapped. Pramila looked gratified and left the stage to take her place among the listeners. The veena player, who had accompanied Pramila, shifted into a meditative mood. The three poets frowned and sweated and thought hard. At last the younger of the Mayans rose to her feet. She signalled to the musicians. The tabla set up a sombre rhythm and the veena seemed almost to wail. She spoke.

> Song of a Grade B Mother
>
> That first wrench hurt —
>   when they took her from me.
> The other mother raised her.
>   Daily she grows
> in strength and beauty;
>   and I,
> who never had her,
>   (yet I made her)
> am as content
>   as is necessary.

The audience sighed and applauded. The tamboura droned. The

second Mayan now stood up. She glanced at the musicians and recited as follows:

> Song of the Grade C Mothers
>
> Other women's children – for whom
> >we care.
> Snotty nosed darlings – dream
> >and despair.
> Shall these daughters grow? We trim
> >and we pare
> the unfinished young we did
> >not bear.

This effort was less well received than the other had been, but still, it was clearly acceptable. There was moderate applause. Jyanvi trembled. What was she supposed to do? She got to her feet so abruptly that the musicians were caught off-guard, but at her first words the tabla sounded ominously. Jyanvi plunged on.

> Song of a Non-Mother
>
> I loved my love with passion.
> She said, 'Will you marry me?'
> I said, 'Is that the fashion?'
> She said, 'It is indeed.'
>
> I cooked and cleaned and scoured.
> I worked myself to the bone.
> Her little children devoured
> my labours every one.
>
> They were clean and quick and sprightly.
> They scampered in the sun.
> 'I must go,' I said politely,
> and left true love alone.

In spite of the preposterous title, the Mayan mothers had let her finish, but now there was a moment of silence. 'In the name of the goddess, clap!' whispered Saraswati. 'Otherwise she's in trouble.' The Blue Donkey and Saraswati led the applause, others joined them; but the Blue Donkey noted that neither Shyamila the Civil, nor the tall hawk-nosed woman who accompanied her, were among those who applauded. Still, for the time being, at least, the crisis had been glossed over. An interval followed. Jyanvi stumbled from the stage and joined the Blue Donkey. Both Saraswati and the Blue Donkey were kind to her, but she seemed numbed and took in little of the rest of the performance.

4

Children are wonderful

The following day Jyanvi was locked up. The Blue Donkey had contrived to get permission to visit her. She looked around. Jyanvi's cell was clean enough. It had a wooden bunk, a small table, a barred window and a concrete floor. For some unknown reason, possibly therapeutic, a potted rose had been placed in a corner, where it was doing its best to look as though it was willing to grow.

'Why am I in prison?' Jyanvi demanded as soon as the Blue Donkey entered her cell.

'You're not in prison,' the Blue Donkey told her. 'They don't have prisons. You're in "hospital". They think you need therapy.'

'What for?'

The Blue Donkey looked at her. Hadn't Jyanvi realised just how much she had offended the Mayans? 'For disliking children,' she replied briefly.

'Oh, come now.' Jyanvi paced up and down. 'All I've ever said is that children, by definition, are unsatisfactory adults, and that they're a lot of work. These women are mothers and they're intelligent. Surely they don't go around saying children are wonderful. After all, they spend half their time making them grow up!'

The Blue Donkey shook her head. 'Don't argue with me,

Jyanvi. I haven't put you here. Try to understand that you're in serious trouble.'

Jyanvi sat down. 'What have I done?' she asked more quietly.

'You've sinned against motherhood – against the core of their identities, their religion, and their family structure. Isn't that enough? I told you to be careful. Have you heard of Asha the Apostate?'

'No. Who was she?'

'Gagri's mother – the Matriarch's eldest daughter. She was exiled for heresy.'

'Oh.' Some of the Blue Donkey's message had at last got through. Jyanvi pulled herself together. 'I'm sorry,' she said. 'What's to be done?'

'Saraswati pleaded for you before the Matriarch. She said that you were a foreigner, that you did not fully understand their codes and conventions, and that perhaps by the same token they had misunderstood yours, that your poem was simply a parody of certain attitudes, or at least that it was intentionally ironic, and that in any case, as everybody knew, poetry was not simply self-expression.'

In spite of herself, Jyanvi smiled. 'What did the Matriarch say?'

'She asked Saraswati what it was exactly that she wanted her to do. Saraswati requested a Special Hearing. She didn't dare ask for anything more.'

For a moment or two Jyanvi remained silent. 'I see,' she said at last. 'Thank you. And please thank Saraswati for me. When is the Special Hearing?'

'At noon, today. The Matriarch herself is likely to preside. Try to think through what you're going to say.'

Jyanvi looked at the Blue Donkey. She folded her arms. 'I shall say that children are wonderful!' she said scornfully.

The Blue Donkey frowned. Had Jyanvi understood the seriousness of her position? 'Oh Jyanvi! Be careful,' she warned. 'I must go now and see if I can get a word with Saraswati before the trial.'

'Trial?' Jyanvi was on her feet again. 'I thought it was a hearing . . .'

When the Blue Donkey had left, Jyanvi walked up and down her cell several times. She noticed that the rose in the corner looked disheartened. She gave it the rest of her drinking water. Then she scowled at it; but the rosebush did not instantly revive, burst into bloom or even say thank you. 'Sensible thing,' Jyanvi muttered. She reseated herself on the wooden bunk and settled down to reconsider her views on mothers and children.

Jyanvi was taken back to the palace by the two policewomen who had brought her to the hospital, members presumably of the Therapists' Guild. She was merely asked to accompany them. There was no suggestion that force might be used. They were large women, kindly, almost maternal. She guessed that if she tried to run, she would be treated like any child and made to do what was good for her. They were not bullies; she was irrational and they were caring for her. Besides, like most children, she knew perfectly well there was nowhere to run. Jyanvi drew herself up and tried to look as grown up as possible.

It was to be a semi-formal hearing. The Matriarch sat in a large chair with Malini Devi and Saraswati on either side, while Shyamila the Civil and Pramila the Poet occupied the flanks. Valerie and the Blue Donkey were confined to the sidelines. Jyanvi faced the semi-circle. 'Like a family gathering,' she thought to herself. 'I, of course, am the outsider.' She greeted them formally.

Shyamila motioned to her to take a chair. Jyanvi sat down. Shyamila began. 'Given the fact that you were a grown-up woman, and in view of your reputation as a poet, we assumed when you came here that you had long ago achieved adult status. That is a matter that must be cleared up. Are you now, or have you ever been, a Grade A, B or C mother?'

'Your Highness, I have been a Grade C mother for fifteen years.' Jyanvi knew that Shyamila was not necessarily entitled to be called Her Highness, but thought that it would please her.

Shyamila's face betrayed nothing, however. She continued

soberly, 'But then why have you never applied for Grade A status or at least Grade B? After fifteen years of service you're entitled to that.'

'Your Highness, due to my age I did not apply for Grade B status. But I did apply for status as a co-mother. Unfortunately, because of the structures of my society, I was rejected on the grounds that a father would be much more useful.'

'What is a "father"?' interrupted Malini Devi.

'In patriarchal societies,' Shyamila explained, 'the pretty boys grow to a larger size and attempt to rule. Many of them then take up, after a fashion, the functions of co-mothers.'

'I see,' murmured Malini Devi, though from the puzzled look on her face it was obvious that she did not see at all.

'And during your fifteen years as a Grade C mother, did you train many daughters and did they grow up into responsible adults?' the Matriarch asked.

'Your Majesty,' replied Jyanvi, 'in our societies the pretty boys are trained alongside our daughters.'

There was a murmur among the Mayans. 'But that must result in chaos!' Malini Devi expostulated.

'Your Ladyship,' Jyanvi answered with a sad smile, 'it frequently does.'

Shyamila the Civil looked thoughtful. 'In that case your Grade C status is highly questionable.'

'If you say so, Your Highness, but might I point out that it was achieved under difficult conditions.' Jyanvi did her best to speak with due deference.

'Yes. She has a point,' the Matriarch intervened. She addressed Jyanvi directly. 'But if you choose to remain in Mayan society, you must have a function and you must have some status. Do you so choose?'

Jyanvi trembled. She had hoped not to have to decide so soon. She searched Saraswati's face. Saraswati seemed to be pleading with her. Jyanvi took a deep breath. 'I so choose,' she said clearly. Her head roared. What had she let herself in for?

'Very well,' she heard Shyamila reply. 'What is your function?'

'I am a poet.' Was that the right answer? Jyanvi didn't know.

Pramila the Poet cleared her throat. 'As Chief of the Guild of Poets it is my duty to inform the present company that there may be some difficulty in admitting Jyanvi as a member of the Guild. There is a controversy over her performance last night. The matter is still under discussion.'

'What else can you do?' Shyamila asked.

'I can teach poetry.' Jyanvi hesitated. 'And I can cook and clean and look after children.'

The Matriarch took matters in hand. 'Very well. You are provisionally admitted to the Guild of Servants as Grade C mother. Should you do well, the question of your status may be reconsidered.'

'But who will employ her?' Malini Devi queried.

Shyamila the Civil looked blank, and Pramila the Poet looked preoccupied. Saraswati tugged at the Matriarch's sari. 'I will employ her,' said the Matriarch at last, 'as personal servant and Grade C mother to Gagri the Good.' She glanced at Jyanvi. 'No doubt your considerable experience will stand you in good stead. You will, of course, be paid.'

For a moment Jyanvi thought that the Matriarch was having a joke at her expense, then she realised that the Matriarch was serious and that she, Jyanvi, was expected to be grateful. 'Thank you,' she murmured.

Later the four of them crowded into the Blue Donkey's room. Jyanvi sat slumped in a corner. Saraswati had her arm about her.

'I told you it doesn't do to displease Pramila the Poet.' Valerie sounded smug. 'Still, I'll do what I can. It will take time to placate her.'

'Will it be my turn next?' asked the Blue Donkey. 'What will they do about my status?'

'You're quite safe,' answered Saraswati, 'provided that what you told me about having taken a vow of celibacy is true, of course.'

'It's true enough, but how is it relevant?'

'Celibates are sacred. They occur so rarely that none of the rules apply to them. You can remain an honoured guest as long as you like, provided you remain asexual. Pramila is thinking of taking her vows.'

'I see,' said the Blue Donkey. 'So I'm all right. But what about Jyanvi? Will she survive?'

Nobody answered.

5

An ordinary woman

Saraswati and Jyanvi walked along the beach. The waves pounded. An obliging moon shone down on them. Saraswati was being kind and tender, but Jyanvi was intent on other matters. She frowned.

'Tell me about money,' she said abruptly, scuffing the sand with her sandal and letting it trickle over her toes.

Her tone jarred, but Saraswati answered amiably enough. 'What do you want to know?'

'Do you have money?'

'Yes, of course.'

'And does everyone have the same amount?' Jyanvi bent down to pick up a cowrie.

'Of course not. It's roughly distributed according to rank.'

'That isn't fair!' Jyanvi's tone verged on the truculent.

'What good is rank if you don't have the money to back it up?' Saraswati was genuinely puzzled.

'And what does a woman's rank depend upon?' Jyanvi demanded.

'On birth and merit. Surely that's obvious,' Saraswati replied. 'Why are you so cross?' She took Jyanvi's arm and though Jyanvi did not shake it off, she turned around to face Saraswati so that Saraswati's arm slipped away.

'I'm not cross! In a just society everyone ought to be equal.' She sounded petulant.

Saraswati tried to take her arm again and unruffle her, but Jyanvi shook her head fiercely. 'No, don't try to soothe me. Just answer a few questions. Don't you see? I've got to understand how things work.'

Saraswati sighed. 'All right,' she agreed. Perhaps Jyanvi's mood would change once her questions had all been answered.

'Right. Now, where does the money come from?'

'From the coffers of the Guilds and the Five Great Families and the Matriarch, of course,' Saraswati replied.

'But where did they get it from?' Jyanvi persisted.

'From the mothers of Maya for services rendered and goods supplied.'

'I see,' said Jyanvi, though she wasn't sure she saw at all. She tried another tack. 'Look, if an ordinary woman – someone like me - decides she needs to make a little money, what does she do? What are the sources of income?'

Saraswati thought for a moment. 'She sells her skills, and then, of course, if she has any children, there are the bonuses that accrue from the children.'

'From the children?'

'Yes. If the children do well, you get paid,' Saraswati explained. 'The bonuses are substantial.'

'And do you have to make a payment to have a child?'

'In some instances. If the state insists that you're a Grade A mother and ought to have a child, then the state pays. This also applies to Grade B mothers. But where the state does not insist, only permits, you have to show that you can pay.' It was like explaining to someone that the sky is blue, Saraswati thought; but she remained patient. 'That's why so many Grade C mothers have to work for years to alter their status,' she added helpfully.

Jyanvi frowned. The whole system seemed very unfair. She felt baffled. She tried once again. 'Do Grade A mothers sometimes raise Grade C daughters?' she asked.

'All mothers who raise daughters have to be Grade A,' Saraswati responded.

'No, I mean the ones who are born Grade A.'

'No one is born Grade A,' Saraswati told her reasonably. 'We have to pass tests.'

But Jyanvi wasn't satisfied. 'No, I mean the ones that are naturally Grade A,' she said doggedly, 'the ones that the state insists ought to have children.'

Saraswati hesitated. 'Well, I suppose it's true that in certain houses there's a high proportion of potential Grade A's. The genes are better, and besides, these Grade A mothers have the resources to hire a number of Grade C mothers. It all helps.'

Saraswati caught Jyanvi's hand. She would have liked a change of subject, but Jyanvi was relentless. 'These houses you speak of, do you mean the Five Great Families and the Matriarchy itself?'

'Yes. But Jyanvi, why do you worry so much about all these things? The Matriarch likes you. If you do well with Gagri the Good, you can apply for Grade A status as co-mother of my own daughter. It will be all right,' Saraswati coaxed.

'But I'm not a mother,' Jyanvi cried passionately. 'I'm a poet!'

'Everyone's a mother,' replied Saraswati placidly. 'As soon as all the fuss subsides, you can re-apply to the Guild of Poets.' She smiled at Jyanvi in a friendly fashion as though to say 'do cheer up'.

Jyanvi attempted to smile back. 'Come on,' she said gruffly. 'Let's walk down to where the sand is wet and look at the waves.' But though the waves rolled in one after another, Jyanvi could not detect a usable pattern.

Gagri the Good was sitting astride the Blue Donkey and pounding her shoulders when Jyanvi returned from fetching a toy.

'Get off!' yelled Jyanvi. She hauled her off the Blue Donkey's back and set her on the ground. The child kicked and screamed and rolled into a puddle.

'I only asked you to mind her for a moment,' Jyanvi reproached the Blue Donkey. 'It wasn't necessary to let her bully you.'

'Oh, I don't mind,' muttered the Blue Donkey.

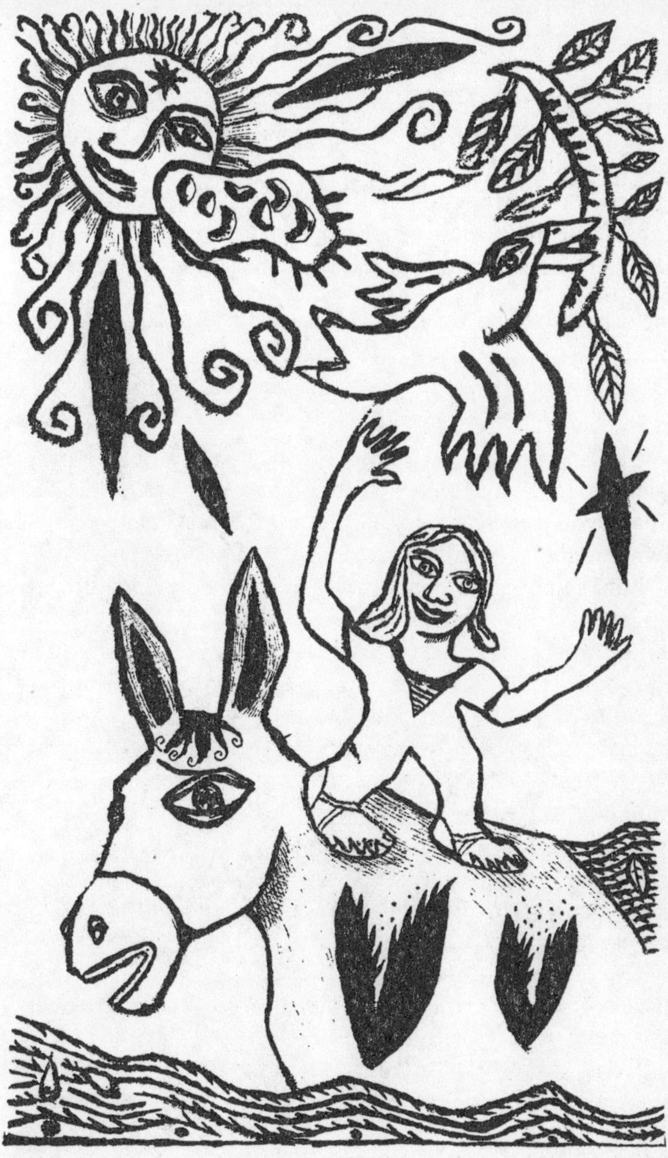

'Well, then I mind. I'm supposed to be responsible for its manners, morals and misdemeanours.'

The Blue Donkey glanced at the small creature, who, by now, was covered in mud. 'What about her appearance?'

'I suppose I'll have to clean her. Come on,' she said to Gagri the Good. The child wouldn't move.

Jyanvi sat down on a bench wearily. 'It's hopeless,' she complained. 'The Matriarch, who is quite clear-headed on every other subject, is utterly contradictory about Gagri the Good.'

'What do you mean?' asked the Blue Donkey gently, though she could make a fair guess at what Jyanvi meant.

'Well, the Matriarch thinks that the child is perfect, and at the same time she thinks it must somehow be made to grow up.'

'And that's a contradiction?' murmured the Blue Donkey.

'Yes. Because a child, by definition, is an imperfect person.'

'Ah.' The Blue Donkey paused. 'Well, the thing is you're supposed to love her,' she suggested cautiously.

'Why should I?' Jyanvi growled.

'Well, if for no other reason,' replied the Blue Donkey, 'then because not to love children, or, at least, to say that you don't, is sacrilege on Maya.'

Jyanvi shrugged. 'Look at it.' She indicated the child. 'It's hardly lovable.'

'Why do you call her "it"?' asked the Blue Donkey.

'Because she's such an amorphous lump!'

'Who will one day grow into a beautiful woman.'

'Yes, another Matriarch brow-beating everyone. Little beast!'

'Well, I don't know about that,' the Blue Donkey protested. 'Try to be nice to her. After all, she has no mother.'

'What do you mean? The whole island is swarming with mothers!'

'Yes, but her real mother, Asha the Apostate, was sent into exile.'

Jyanvi remained unimpressed. 'The Matriarch more than makes it up to her.'

'Try to be nice,' the Blue Donkey repeated. 'Sometimes bribes succeed where threats don't work.'

'I've tried all that,' answered Jyanvi. 'She's used to people being nice to her. She takes it as her due. Besides, she knows damn well that the real source of power lies with the Matriarch. When she wants anything, she just asks her.'

'Well, look,' said the Blue Donkey reasonably, 'whether you like it or not, you've got to get on with Gagri the Good. Otherwise you're done for.'

'Yes, I know.' Jyanvi got to her feet and tried to pick up Gagri bodily. The child bit her. Jyanvi barely stopped herself from giving her a whack.

The Blue Donkey decided she had better intervene. 'Come on,' she said to the child kindly. 'I'll give you a ride so that you can get cleaned up.' The child leaped on to the Blue Donkey's back.

'Wonderful!' muttered Jyanvi. 'First they're horrid and then you reward them for being a little less so!'

'Well, children aren't rational,' returned the Blue Donkey apologetically. 'You'll have to be patient.'

'They're little egoists!' Jyanvi was raging. 'Why don't I just quit and let the Mayans do their worst?'

'Come now, be reasonable,' cajoled the Blue Donkey. 'See, Gagri the Good is going to be good now, aren't you, Gagri?'

'Yes,' replied Gagri smugly. 'I'm always good.'

Jyanvi snorted. The Blue Donkey looked at her warningly. 'Please, Jyanvi, you've got to survive. Pramila the Poet has agreed to let you re-apply to the Guild of Poets. They want you to submit a brand new piece as soon as possible. Can you do it?'

'When?' asked Jyanvi. 'As Gagri's personal servant I feed her my life. When is there time?'

'But you must, Jyanvi. Do calm down and try to be sensible. Once your skills have been reclassified, you'll be free again and can live with Saraswati as co-mother with Grade A status.' The Blue Donkey's voice trailed away.

'Yes,' said Jyanvi. She shuddered.

The children played in Malini Devi's garden. Saraswati and Jyanvi sat in a bower. Creepers of jai, jui and jasmine trailed above them. The scene ought to have been romantic, or at least idyllic, but the children kept interrupting them. Sona was younger than Gagri. There were petty disputes and the formation and dissolution of alliances. During the intervals when the children didn't interrupt, they still remained the centre of focus. Jyanvi's jaws ached with tension.

The Blue Donkey had told Saraswati about Jyanvi's difficulties. Saraswati was trying to help, but she felt uncertain about how to broach the subject.

'Gagri is only eight, you know,' Saraswati began.

Jyanvi did not reply.

'She's not really a bad child, just a little difficult, and must be handled with care. A promising child.'

Jyanvi turned on Saraswati. 'Even you don't seem to understand that I'm not really interested in the welfare of the child. What I'm really interested in is my own welfare. And it seems unreasonable that my life and time should be given up to the wretched child. If she wishes to flourish, let her flourish – at somebody else's expense.'

'But the Matriarch helped you when you were in trouble,' Saraswati pointed out.

'And in return for that must I chop up my life and toss it in gobbets to the hungry child?'

Saraswati recoiled from the vehemence in Jyanvi's voice. 'Jyanvi, surely you're being excessively dramatic. Do you dislike children?'

'Yes! They take everything and give nothing. They're greedy monsters.'

Saraswati glanced involuntarily at her own daughter. Her face softened. 'But they're only children,' she said reasonably. 'If I may say so, I think the mistake you make with young Gagri is that you expect her to behave like a miniature adult.'

'I don't! Her behaviour would be wholly intolerable in a grown-up woman.'

'Yes, that's what I mean. She's only a child.'

'Yes, an imperfect adult. But she demands services and privileges that even adults haven't got, and on top of that she has none of the duties and responsibilities of a real adult.'

'But that's my point.' Saraswati couldn't understand why it all made Jyanvi so furious. 'She's not an adult.'

'What's that to me?'

'Well, yes, but she has to be looked after,' Saraswati responded.

'Then let her behave like a proper dependant,' Jyanvi decreed, 'and say "yes" and "no" and try to be grateful.'

Saraswati was doing her best to understand Jyanvi's point of view. 'But surely the powerlessness of children isn't quite like the powerlessness of anyone else,' she ventured. 'We wanted them, we had them. None of them asked to be born.'

But Jyanvi refused to give weight to the argument. 'If they dislike having been born, there's a remedy available.'

Saraswati was shocked. 'That's harsh!' she exclaimed.

'I did not ask to have Gagri the Good or any other children,' Jyanvi declared.

'But what about society? What about the future?' Saraswati protested. She was trying hard to remain patient.

'What about it?' Jyanvi replied.

'It's the duty of every Mayan to sacrifice herself for the welfare of the children,' Saraswati murmured.

'And what about the children?'

'They, in turn, sacrifice themselves,' Saraswati replied.

'Don't any escape?'

The bitterness in her voice startled Saraswati, but Saraswati was now on surer ground. 'No Mayan would want to escape,' she said quietly.

'Yes, but there's still a lot of hypocrisy about,' Jyanvi muttered.

'What do you mean?'

'Well, the Matriarch's responsible for Gagri the Good, isn't she?' Jyanvi demanded.

'Yes, but what has that to do with it?'

'I don't see the Matriarch sacrificing herself!' Jyanvi retorted.

'But she loves the child! Even her enemies would concede that!' Saraswati had been getting increasingly annoyed. She drew herself up. 'By the way, please remember, you're now discussing my biological mother.'

'Oh, I like and respect her,' Jyanvi replied. 'But can't we at least try to be honest? Can't you see that the more powerful mothers hire other women to care for their children? The more powerful the mother, the more privileged the child.'

'But why does it make you so angry?' Saraswati was perplexed. 'Surely it's natural that a mother should want the best for her child?'

'At the expense of other women,' Jyanvi pointed out. 'If being a mother is such a marvellous thing, why do they pass off the chores to others?'

'Every mother does the best she can for her own children,' Saraswati murmured. What was it that Jyanvi was finding so very difficult?

'And what about the children of other mothers?'

'Well, naturally a mother loves her own children best. Why shouldn't she? But every woman on Maya is a caring mother,' Saraswati explained. 'I don't understand why it makes you so cross. To be allowed to care for a Mayan daughter is a great privilege.'

Jyanvi threw her hands into the air and got up suddenly. 'That's exactly what makes me so cross. The hypocrisy of it all. To be allowed to slave for a snivelling child is not a privilege, it's a bloody bore!'

By now Saraswati was angry and upset. She rose to her feet. 'I see clearly that I misunderstood you. To help me look after my child would not be a privilege for you, but only, as you put it, a bloody bore.'

'But can't you see that it's you I want, not your damn daughter!' Jyanvi was beside herself.

For some reason this mollified Saraswati. 'I see,' she said, 'so you do want me?'

'Yes.'

'Well, then be reasonable. We are not just two women who

can live by ourselves, we are members of a society with a part to perform.' Why couldn't Jyanvi see the obvious?

'And as members of this society we must pay our dues by raising children?'

'If you want to put it that way, yes,' Saraswati replied.

'I see.' Jyanvi sat down. 'And are there any ways of making the tasks of mothering a little easier?'

Saraswati looked at Jyanvi sharply. 'What do you mean?'

'I mean hiring the services of Grade C mothers, for example.'

'Well yes.' Saraswati hesitated. 'I mean it's good for the children. They all go to school where the Grade C mothers are paid to teach them.'

For a while Jyanvi said nothing. At last Saraswati asked, 'Jyanvi, what are you thinking? You're not going to do anything silly, are you?'

'No, I'm just figuring out how to get Grade A status.'

Saraswati looked hurt. 'Is that all you want?'

'No, I want to write verse, and I want you. But I also want my life, you know.'

The children played. The two women remained silent.

After a while Jyanvi said, 'There's a favour I wanted to ask you.'

'Yes, certainly. What is it?'

'There's a potted rose in that damned cell I was locked up in. Could you get it for me, please?'

'Yes, I suppose it could be arranged.' Saraswati was surprised. 'Why do you want it?'

'In order to congratulate it,' Jyanvi replied, 'on having gained its freedom without the necessity of having to be grateful.'

6

A little preview

Ordinarily the testing would have been done at the Training Centre, but as a favour to Shyamila an exception was made for Gagri the Good. As a further concession, the Chief of the Guild of the Servants of the Goddess had decided to conduct the examination herself. Sarla Devi, with her hawk nose and her cold grey eyes, exuded authority. She had swept in, and with the briefest of nods to the Matriarch and only a small smile for Shyamila, had made it quite clear from the outset that she, in her capacity as Examiner, was in sole charge. The Matriarch and Gagri's aunts had been told that they could watch, but only from a distance, and they must not in any way interfere. They were seated in a row against a wall, and Jyanvi, Valerie and the Blue Donkey stood beside them.

The Examiner's assistant was setting out equipment on a large table in the centre of the room. She had several cases, some pots and pans, and, among other items, an enamel basin. Gagri the Good was watching her. Having done her job, the assistant gave Gagri a friendly wink and retired to a corner of the room. Gagri the Good was left face to face with the Examiner. The Examiner opened one of the smaller cases and took out a wooden doll.

'Now,' said the Examiner. 'Here is a doll. Her name is Suman. You are supposed to look after her. What is the first thing you are going to do?'

Gagri looked up at the Examiner. She was scrubbed and clean and had on a brocaded blouse and skirt. She knew she was supposed to give the right answer, but she didn't know what the right answer was.

'What are you going to do?' The Examiner was insistent.

'I'm going to put her to bed and send her to sleep. Then I'm going out to play,' replied Gagri the Good.

'But the doll isn't sleepy. The doll is crying. The doll is crying very loudly. What are you going to do?'

'Well,' Gagri the Good thought for a second, 'I'll just tell her to stop crying. Stop crying,' she said to the doll.

'The doll hasn't stopped crying,' the Examiner informed Gagri the Good.

'I'll just put her to bed then.' Gagri was getting bored. 'In the end she'll stop crying and go to sleep.' She seized the doll and put her down horizontally.

'No,' said the Examiner. 'The doll is hungry. If she goes on crying, she'll make herself sick. What are you going to do?'

Gagri the Good looked exasperated. 'If the doll is hungry, why doesn't she eat? Why do you ask me what I'm going to do?'

'The doll is too little to feed herself. You'll have to give her some food.'

'All right,' agreed Gagri the Good impatiently. 'I'll give her some food, but then she had better go to sleep, because I want to go out and play.' She looked around. 'What does it eat?' she asked the Examiner.

'Boiled milk.'

'Have we got any milk?'

'Yes, but you'll have to boil it first and then cool it down so that the doll can drink it.'

For a moment everyone thought that Gagri the Good was about to revolt, but the Matriarch had warned her that the one thing she mustn't say was that she wouldn't. Suddenly she brightened. 'But it's all make believe.' She waved her hand. 'There, the milk has been boiled.' She waved her hand again. 'Now, it's cooled down.' She picked up the doll and pretended to feed it. 'The doll has been fed. Now it's gone to sleep and I'm going out.'

The Matriarch smiled broadly, and even Jyanvi was amused. 'Clever devil,' she muttered to herself, but the Examiner remained impassive.

'No,' she said to Gagri the Good. 'As you say, that was make believe, now see what you can do with a real one.' With that the Examiner opened another case – it was padded and equipped with air holes – and produced a baby.

When Jyanvi realised that the baby was real, she started forward. Valerie restrained her. 'Don't,' she whispered. 'Don't interfere. Otherwise Gagri will be disqualified. It's one of the pretty boys. He'll be all right.'

Gagri gaped. The baby was filthy. Its nose ran. It had soiled its clothes. The Examiner held it out to her. 'There,' said the Examiner. 'What do you think of it?'

'It's dirty,' Gagri's voice was barely above a whisper.

The Examiner thrust it into Gagri's arms. 'Well, then you'll have to clean it, won't you?'

Gagri clutched the baby. The baby howled. Gagri clutched the baby harder; the baby's howling increased in volume. Gagri looked up despairingly. 'How?'

'First you must put it down on the table carefully, and then you must take off its clothes.'

Gagri put down the baby carefully and struggled with its clothes. They fell to the floor in a dirty heap. 'Now what?' Gagri stared at the wriggling baby, terrified that it would roll off the table.

'Now you must bathe it.'

With the help of the Examiner's assistant the baby was put in the basin, washed, dried and dressed in clean clothes. Through all these operations it had cried unceasingly. Gagri looked at the Examiner in a daze. 'Is it over?' she asked.

'No. Now it must be fed.'

'Boiled milk?'

'Yes. Here is a bottle.' The Examiner nodded to her assistant to give Gagri a bottle. Gagri fed the baby. The baby smiled. For a moment Gagri felt triumphant. Then the baby wet its nappy. With the help of the assistant Gagri changed it. 'Now will it sleep?' she asked the Examiner.

'Yes,' said the Examiner. 'It will sleep for a while.' The assistant lifted it into its crib and shut the lid, and retired again into the background.

'Pick up its clothes and put them into this basket,' the Examiner directed Gagri.

Gagri looked at the pile with distaste, but did as she was told. Then she looked up at the Examiner. Had she done well? After all, she had done everything she was told to do. But the Examiner only said casually, 'You may go.' Gagri the Good ran straight towards the Matriarch; but the Matriarch shook her head at her and Gagri swerved and ran out of the room.

The Matriarch and her daughters surged forward. But Sarla Devi was supervising the packing of the equipment. She kept them waiting. 'Did she pass?' asked the Matriarch anxiously. Sarla Devi looked into the Ranisaheb's eyes for a second. 'Just. She'll do.' Shyamila the Civil stepped forward. She took Sarla Devi's arm. For a moment Sarla Devi hesitated, then she linked arms and together they walked out.

There was great celebration in the palace that day, rituals and ceremonies to mark the passing of Gagri's First Test. The goddess was worshipped with milk and honey and garlands of flowers. In a week or two Gagri the Good would be sent to school and the Matriarch would receive a substantial bonus.

Jyanvi walked away thoughtfully. The Blue Donkey caught up with her in an inner courtyard. She was contemplating a spindly rosebush. 'Do you think it will thrive?' she asked gloomily.

'Yes, why not?' the Blue Donkey replied. 'There's plenty of light and it's sheltered here. Listen. Tonight would be a good evening for a little preview of the piece you're presenting to the Poet's Guild. Saraswati has made sure you're dining with the family.'

Jyanvi looked at the Blue Donkey in amazement. 'But I haven't written it.'

'Write it this afternoon.'
'How can I? I have to mind the child.'
'I'll mind her for you. But write that piece. And Jyanvi – '
'Yes?'
'It would be appropriate if it somehow commemorated Gagri's success.'

The Ranisaheb and her daughters had flung shawls around their shoulders. The weather had turned cooler. Jyanvi was reminded of her first evening at the palace. Had anything changed? Did she know a little more? She felt sad and uncertain, though everyone else was in a good mood. Saraswati kept giving her encouraging little glances, but Jyanvi kept her eyes down, not really knowing how to respond. The Blue Donkey nudged Jyanvi. 'Have you written it?' she whispered urgently.

'Yes, but – '

'All right, then. This is your chance. Gagri goes to school in a few days. The Matriarch is in a good mood.' The Blue Donkey signalled to Saraswati; and as soon as the opportunity arose, Saraswati said, 'I believe Jyanvi has a poem she would like to read to us.'

The Ranisaheb smiled her permission, Pramila asked whether it was rhymed and Shyamila tried to look interested though it was apparent her thoughts were elsewhere.

'It's a story,' said Jyanvi.

'To mark the occasion,' added the Blue Donkey helpfully.

'What is the title?' enquired the Matriarch.

The Matriarch was being exceptionally affable. Jyanvi realised that the old woman had been genuinely worried about Gagri's test. 'Well, perhaps she's human,' Jyanvi muttered to herself. Aloud she said, 'It hasn't got a title yet, Your Highness.'

'Well, read it. Perhaps we can help you find a title.'

With that Jyanvi read out the following story:

'It so happened that there was once a young woman who did not want to have a daughter. This was her secret and her secret was so dreadful that she kept it to herself. But her genes were good, her background irreproachable, and she herself was not unintelligent, so that it is not surprising that she passed all her tests and was accordingly given Grade A status. It was requested of her that she bear a daughter. There was no help for it, she had to exercise her privilege. During the long months of pregnancy, the young woman prayed day and night and invoked the help of the Great Goddess. Now the ways of the goddess are hard to understand and it isn't entirely clear what it was for that the young woman prayed. Whatever the mystery behind the matter, the fact remains that as soon as the young woman's daughter was born, the child spoke and apologised to her mother that she was as yet so entirely helpless. It was apparent at once that the child was a prodigy and had somehow been born with the wisdom and experience of the goddess herself. In a day or two she was walking about, within a week she was feeding herself, and within two weeks she had taken over the management of the entire household and was feeding her mother and herself. They named her Shanta, because despite all her abilities she was gentle and peaceful. The mothers of Maya watched in amazement this strange reversal of the roles proper to mother and daughter; for as Shanta Devi grew in power, her mother declined in strength and health, and at the end of four weeks the mother was dead. 'What does it mean?' the mothers of Maya asked one another. They felt afraid. Only Shanta Devi remained unperturbed. With her customary calm she performed the rites for her mother's funeral, and when the pyre had been lit, she faced the populace. 'What does it mean?' the mothers of Maya demanded of her. 'Are you a Destroyer? Do you carry death?' But Shanta Devi only smiled. 'You know in your hearts exactly what it means. Within a fortnight I, too, shall be dead.' And that is what happened. The mothers of Maya declared her a saint and they built a shrine to honour her, but for weeks afterwards they would look anxiously at their own daughters to make sure that they, at least, were not racing ahead.'

Jyanvi stopped. Pramila the Poet looked puzzled. 'The meaning is a little obscure,' she commented. Shyamila the Civil said nothing, but a slight frown had appeared on her forehead. The

Matriarch's expression was unreadable. Saraswati and the Blue Donkey trembled for Jyanvi.

'So you call yourself a poet?' the Matriarch demanded.

'Yes, Your Highness.'

'And you wrote this tale to please me?'

'Well – '

'But it does not please.'

'No, Your Highness.'

'On the other hand, it does contain an element of truth.'

Jyanvi relaxed a fraction, but the Matriarch wasn't done with her. 'What is the function of poets?'

'To tell the truth, Your Highness.'

'And do they know the truth?'

'Whatever little they know, Your Highness.'

'And is the truth useful?'

'I don't know, Your Highness.'

'You don't know!' returned the Matriarch. 'Has anyone told you you were a fool?'

Pramila felt it was time for her to say something in her capacity as Chief of Poets. 'I fear,' she began, 'that you have misunderstood the nature of poetry . . .'

But the Ranisaheb cut her short. 'Be quiet, Pramila. I have said she was a fool; she is also a poet. You will admit her to the Guild. I herewith appoint her my Personal Poet.' She turned to Jyanvi. 'You will wait on me in my dressing chamber tomorrow at eight.'

Shyamila the Civil rose to her feet. 'Mother, if you're dispensing favours tonight, surely it ought to be remembered that it's to the Guild of the Goddess' Servants that we're greatly obligated?'

The Matriarch looked at Shyamila. 'Are you suggesting that without Sarla Devi, Gagri the Good would have failed the test?'

Shyamila looked away. 'Well, no,' she mumbled. Then she rallied. 'But if you are bending the rules, surely you might bend them in a worthier cause?' She said this with some indignation, and regretted it instantly.

The Matriarch's mood had changed. 'It was you and Sarla

Devi who were foremost in insisting on the letter of the law when Gagri's mother was exiled,' she said.

Pramila sucked in her breath. It was the first time since her eldest sister had been sent away that the Matriarch had referred to the event. The Blue Donkey tried to think of something harmless to say, but the Matriarch was speaking again. She glanced at the company. 'You tire me,' she said.

They had all been dismissed. They dispersed uncertainly, and the Ranisaheb went to bed.

7

Well, Poet?

The Ranisaheb was combing her hair. She had washed it that morning with coconut milk, coconut oil and natural soap, and had had it dried above a coal fire with incense. Jyanvi could still smell the incense. A servant was carrying away the little iron stove which contained the coals. Jyanvi looked at the Matriarch and saw an aged woman, excessively overweight, excessively determined. Then she noticed the fine hands, the thinning hair and the lines on her face. For a moment she liked her enormously, but the feeling soon passed as the Matriarch addressed her.

'Well, Poet? And what varnished truth can you offer today?'

'Varnished, Your Highness?' Jyanvi queried. She was on her guard and wasn't going to risk giving offence.

'Yes. Varnished,' the Matriarch repeated. 'Any fool can tell the truth, and, at court, only a fool sometimes does. It's the varnish that distinguishes fool from poet.'

The Matriarch seemed to be in a good mood, but Jyanvi was being careful. 'I hadn't thought of that, Your Highness,' was all she said.

'Well, now that I've told you something about the nature of poets,' the Matriarch continued, 'it's your turn to tell me something about the nature of matriarchs.' The Matriarch finished tying her hair in a bun, stuck in a few pins and looked quizzically at her personal poet. Jyanvi had remained standing, not having been given permission to sit down as yet.

Jyanvi replied gravely, 'To be a matriarch is a difficult task, filled with responsibility. It needs the wisdom and experience, which, happily for Maya, Your Highness possesses.'

But to this the Matriarch responded with disgust. 'Any courtier could have told me that. In fact, most of them do at least once a day. Pull yourself together, woman. You sound like a parrot. I asked for a poet.' She got up, examined the saris laid out for her and picked up one. She unfolded it, held it against herself briefly, glanced in the mirror and let it drop to the ground. Then she selected a dark green one with its matching blouse. She put on the blouse and began tucking the sari into her petticoat.

While the Ranisaheb pleated and tucked and draped the sari around herself, Jyanvi had had a chance to think, but she didn't know what to say. At last she mumbled, 'Your Highness, I'm only a poet sometimes, that is, during those moments when I compose a poem. I can't turn it on and off.'

The Matriarch looked her full in the face. 'And am I the Matriarch only sometimes? Well? Tell me that! Can I turn it on and off?' She began to stamp on the edge of her sari in order to make the length even.

Jyanvi answered slowly, 'No, Your Highness, you can't turn it off.' She found she was kneeling at the Matriarch's feet trying to help her adjust the length.

'So. You can't switch on, and I can't switch off. And why is that? Can you tell me that?' the Matriarch demanded.

Jyanvi rose to her feet. 'Because, Your Highness, the institutions of Maya are too well made.'

The Ranisaheb chuckled. 'That will do. Sit down. A truth a day. You're earning your keep. What's the going rate for poets?'

Suddenly Jyanvi realized that the old woman was having a game with her. She ventured a smile. 'Payment is generally for keeping quiet or telling lies. A monarch who pays for the truth is like – '

'A poet who does not complain. In other words, a rarity.

Now. Today is the Day of Oracles. We're going to the Cave Temple. Saraswati will be accompanying us.' The Matriarch paused and when she saw Jyanvi brighten, she added thoughtfully, 'Our kinship system is complex, as you know. In future you may call me Aisaheb.'

Jyanvi wasn't quite sure what to make of it. 'Thank you,' she said.

The Matriarch smiled. 'Oh, and go and find the Blue Donkey. On the Day of Oracles the Matriarch of Maya receives instructions from the goddess herself. These instructions are sometimes hard to interpret.'

Though mystified, Jyanvi hurried off on the Matriarch's errand. She found Valerie and the Blue Donkey with Gagri the Good in the coconut grove. Gagri was up a tree again. Jyanvi almost felt sorry for her. All this must soon end.

'The Aisaheb would like you to accompany us to the Cave Temple,' she informed the Blue Donkey.

'Who's the Aisaheb?' asked the Blue Donkey.

'The Matriarch. She told me to call her Aisaheb,' Jyanvi replied.

Valerie had been listening intently. 'Do you know what that means?' She had an odd expression on her face.

'Well, "Ai" means "mother" and "Saheb" means "Ladyship" or "Mistress". I thought it meant she was pleased with me.' Jyanvi looked anxious. 'Does it mean something else?'

'It means' – Valerie pronounced each word distinctly – 'that she has decided to become your Matron.'

'Oh.' In spite of herself Jyanvi felt a smile spread across her face.

'You're lucky,' went on Valerie. 'It comes of being a lesbian, I suppose. It's easy for you. You relate to women. It took me a long time just to adjust.' She could not quite suppress a trace of envy, but she did her best. 'Anyhow, well done!' she said.

Just then Gagri the Good let a coconut drop. 'Hey! Look at me!'

The Blue Donkey answered automatically, 'Be careful, dear.'

Then she turned to Valerie again. 'Are you heterosexual?' she enquired carefully.

'Yes. Yes, of course, I am,' Valerie replied. She felt a sudden urge to confide in the Blue Donkey. 'You don't know what a relief it is to talk to someone who actually understands what the word means!'

'Yes, it must be difficult,' the Blue Donkey murmured sympathetically. 'Aren't there any men at all on Maya Diip?'

'No. Not that I have much use for men, but, well – ' Valerie broke off.

'What about the pretty boys?' enquired the Blue Donkey.

'That would be like having sex with children or perhaps with creatures of a different species. The mothers of Maya would put me in jail!' Valerie replied. 'But it's not just the sex,' Valerie continued. 'It's – it's the Mayan attitude. They don't seem to understand or even want to understand who I am or what I've been.'

'It must have been very hard to fit into Mayan society,' said the Blue Donkey understandingly. 'You've done very well. But tell me, how do the mothers conceive their children?'

'They milk the pretty boys.'

'What?' asked Jyanvi and the Blue Donkey simultaneously.

'They milk them of semen before the boys dive into the sea and turn into foam,' Valerie elaborated.

'This "turning into foam" – ' Jyanvi hesitated. It was a question which had been troubling her for some time now. 'Is that a euphemism or – ?'

'Well, sort of.' Valerie grimaced. 'The thing is that the pretty boys go mad at fourteen.'

'What do you mean?'

'Well, they become aggressive. They fight . . .' It was a subject she obviously found distasteful, but Jyanvi and the Blue Donkey were thoroughly intrigued.

'That sounds fairly normal for boys that age,' Jyanvi put in.

Valerie looked at her. 'Boys aren't the norm on Maya Diip. The boys fight among themselves. The mothers of Maya let them. Eventually there's nothing left to fight, only the waves. So they fight the waves, turn into foam, so to speak . . .'

'What a waste,' Jyanvi couldn't help saying.

'Well, Asha the Apostate protested,' Valerie said wearily, 'and look what happened to her. The Mayans say that to keep the pretty boys alive would be even more wasteful. You see, the Mayans think that except for the semen the lives of pretty boys are perfectly pointless.'

'Why don't the pretty boys turn against the mothers?' Jyanvi asked.

'I don't know. I suppose because they're not organised and haven't any weapons. They turn most of their aggression against themselves. Besides, there aren't very many. The mothers of Maya don't regard them as their own children – just as necessities.' Valerie shrugged. 'That was the Princess Asha's point. She went around saying that if they were treated differently, they might be different. According to her, they would never reach the stature of normal women, but that, perhaps within their limitations, they could be helped to grow up.'

During Valerie's explanation, Gagri the Good had slithered down the tree and crept up behind them. She had meant to give them a start, but she stopped when she caught her mother's name.

'It wouldn't be much fun being a man on Maya,' Jyanvi muttered. She hesitated. 'If you don't like it here, why did you stay?' she asked Valerie.

'Because it's even less fun being a woman Outside!'

'Could you have gone with the Princess Asha?' enquired the Blue Donkey.

'I suppose so, but to what purpose? She was sent off into the forest.'

'Did she have much support?'

'No, not much, but she had a little. I suppose that's why she was exiled.'

'Do you mean she was exiled by her own mother?' Jyanvi asked.

'I'm not sure,' Valerie replied thoughtfully. 'I don't think the

Matriarch had much choice. You see, the Guild of the Servants of the Goddess declared her a heretic and the Therapists' Guild pronounced her incurable... Shyamila and Sarla Devi had a hand in it.'

'But didn't the Matriarch mind?' Jyanvi persisted.

'Well, it's hard to say. Look, it's a forbidden subject, and really I shouldn't have said anything. Last night was the first time I heard the Matriarch mention it.' Valerie was looking extremely uneasy.

'Boo!' Gagri, unable to understand what the grown-ups were saying, had got tired of eavesdropping.

Valerie jumped. Jyanvi shouted. And the Blue Donkey said to Gagri gently, 'You mustn't do that, dear.'

Gagri squirmed and grinned. 'Look at all the coconuts I got!'

'That was very clever, dear.'

'Yes, I am clever,' Gagri agreed, and went off to try and pick up all the coconuts at once.

'Thank you for telling us all these things,' the Blue Donkey said to Valerie soberly. 'Just one more question. Why do they call the pretty boys "pretty"?'

'Out of kindness,' Valerie replied.

8

Day of Oracles

They had driven to the top of the cliff. There the Chief of the Guild of the Servants of the Goddess, together with her acolytes, awaited them. Sarla Devi greeted the Matriarch with formal politeness. She glanced at the Matriarch's entourage. 'Has the Princess Shyamila not accompanied you?' she asked the Matriarch. She kept her voice carefully uninflected.

'No,' replied the Matriarch. 'The Princess Shyamila has not accompanied us.' She offered no explanation.

'I see,' replied the Chief Servant of the Goddess.

On the face of it there had been nothing sinister in this brief interchange, but Jyanvi felt nervous. Behind them the sea pounded against the cliffs. Below them a crowd of Mayans had gathered to watch the Matriarch descend to the Cave Temple. When the Matriarch re-emerged, she would have the answers to the questions which most troubled the Mayans at present. Each of the mothers had sent her question to the Goddess' Guild, and with the aid of a computer the Servants of the Goddess had picked out the three most frequently asked. The process was supposed to be entirely automated, but Sarla Devi's grey eyes glinted as she presented the Matriarch with the 'Important Three'. The Matriarch took them and waved them at the crowd. The crowd cheered. Then the Matriarch read them out:

'1. Who will be the Matriarch's Successor?
2. Will Maya Diip prosper for ever?
3. Under what circumstances may a Mayan mother disobey the Mayan Law?'

The crowd sighed, the drums thundered. Jyanvi could just see the cave mouth halfway down the cliff. Led by the Servants of the Goddess, the slow descent to the cave began. At the cave mouth, when it looked as though Sarla Devi was about to guide them further, the Matriarch paused and thanked her. The Servants of the Goddess had to remain outside. It was obvious that Sarla Devi didn't like it at all, but to enter the Cave with her chosen companions was the Matriarch's prerogative on the Day of Oracles.

Saraswati now led the way through a short corridor. Daylight streamed in from the other end. They found themselves in an open space in the centre of which was a large temple. The walls of the cliff rose up around them. Towards the top, the side facing the sea had been broken off, and it was through this opening that daylight entered. Jyanvi and the Blue Donkey looked around in astonishment. Every square inch of rock had been polished and carved.

'The carvings depict the exploits of the goddess,' Saraswati explained.

Jyanvi felt dazed. The goddess was everywhere, depicted among her friends, her lovers, her warriors, her servants, her enemies and her babies. And she was there in all her aspects: grim, giddy, tender and maternal, languid and luxurious, asleep and waking, austere and amorous, warlike and proud. She was made manifest in time and comprehended it. Jyanvi ran her fingers over the granite. This was stone made flesh. She was overwhelmed.

Before Jyanvi and the Blue Donkey could say anything, the Matriarch spoke. 'You remember the three questions that exercise the minds of the Mayan mothers? Come with me now into the inner temple and we will meditate there and seek guidance.' Her eyes held theirs so that they felt there was something they ought to understand. Saraswati's nod in the direction of the entrance made matters clearer. Without further questions, Jyanvi and the Blue Donkey followed the Matriarch.

The inner temple was dominated by a figure of the goddess dancing. They touched her feet, and lit the lamps set down before her. They they sat down and contemplated the goddess. The limbs moved and did not move. The pattern had been caught, held in motion.

After a while, they heard the Matriarch ask, 'Has the goddess spoken?'

It was Jyanvi who answered.

> 'She who shall reign in the goddess' name
> must suffer change, yet stay the same.'

The Matriarch looked at Jyanvi sharply, and then looked away. 'Interpret it,' she commanded the Blue Donkey.

'Well, Your Majesty,' the Blue Donkey replied, 'your daughter, Saraswati, bears the goddess' name, or at least one of her names. And she was sent away to be adopted by Malini Devi. She has suffered change, yet she remains your daughter in her fidelity and affection and resemblance to you.'

'Yes, I see,' responded the Matriarch thoughtfully. She now looked at Saraswati for a long time. Saraswati held her mother's gaze. At last, the Matriarch spoke. 'So be it.'

Jyanvi was startled. Could the future be fixed so easily? But the Matriarch had already moved on to the next question. 'And shall Maya Diip prosper for ever?' she asked the Blue Donkey.

The Blue Donkey considered for a moment. The lamplight slid along her coat and seemed to caress her. 'The Mayan Lamp shall remain undimmed,' she told the Matriarch, 'till the Daughters of Maya forget their heritage and there are no more mothers, only daughters.'

'But that can never happen!' Saraswati exclaimed.

'Do you think so?' The Matriarch's voice was indulgent. 'The goddess has vouchsafed you a good answer,' she said to the Blue Donkey. 'And now, my dear,' she turned to Saraswati again, 'when you are Matriarch, under what circumstances will you allow a Mayan to disobey the laws of this island?'

'When you are Matriarch.' The words reverberated in Saraswati's head. She took up the challenge and answered steadily, 'When that Mayan ceases to be a Mayan.'

As they heard this, Jyanvi and the Blue Donkey suddenly felt cold. It was only a draught, the lamps had flickered; but they knew that the situation on Maya had changed. Soon, the mothers of Maya would hear the instructions of the goddess. Decisions had been made. They, Jyanvi and the Blue Donkey, had helped to make them. They had not been co-opted, let alone coerced. And yet to have their words become a part of a functioning structure seemed strange, and somehow uncomfortable. Perhaps they had been co-opted? But they had been glad to accompany the Matriarch. The problem of the Oracles had only been a challenge. They had found the words that would fit in gracefully. Shouldn't they be pleased? Surely poetry ought to make things happen? In their hearts both Jyanvi and the Blue Donkey felt uneasy. But the Matriarch had risen. They followed her.

There was the long slow climb back to the summit. In the broad daylight Jyanvi blinked. Sarla Devi's bearing was impeccably correct – and antagonistic. She set the pace relentlessly. The Matriarch was forced to pause for breath. Jyanvi felt concerned, and then silly. Was there any real need to worry about the Matriarch? Hadn't the old lady just manipulated them? It had been done with such ease.

When they reached the summit, a great cry rose up from the crowd. The Matriarch presented them with a moving combination of majesty and humility. The instructions of the goddess were given to the mothers. They cheered and roared. They rode on the crest of Mayan pride, and it was their own beings that made up the wave they were riding upon. Saraswati had always been popular, but they saw her now as her Mother's Daughter and the two together as the supreme embodiment of their noblest dream. The Day of Oracles had been a great success. Only the Servants of the Goddess seemed less than gratified.

PART II

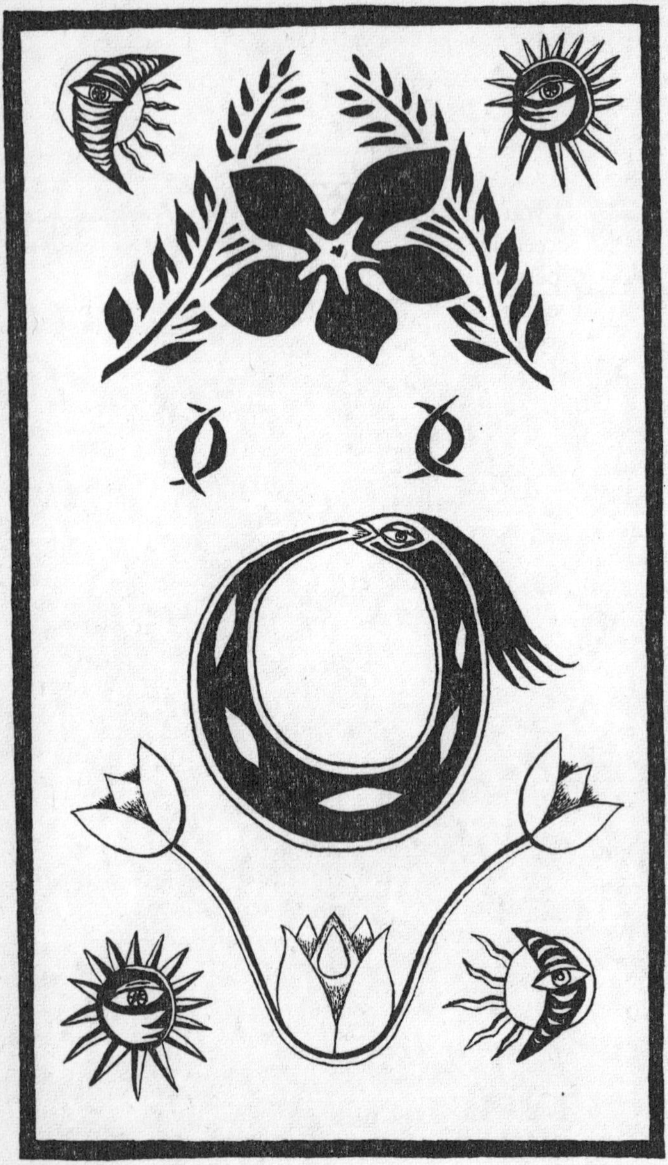

'Did you succeed?' enquired the Cheshire Cat.
'Succeed in what?'
'In persuading the mouse that I'm essentially quite an amiable cat.' Then it did a slow fadeout.

9

Being Eater or Eaten

In the forest there was nothing to do. No creature harmed them. The birds and beasts were amiable enough, and the trees provided food for everyone. Shyamila the Civil, not quite able to bring herself to the point of matricide, had exiled them. The Matriarch and Saraswati had been made to retire and Jyanvi and the Blue Donkey were told to accompany them. Gagri the Good and Saraswati's daughter had been left behind, presumably as hostages.

The trouble had begun as soon as the Matriarch had returned to the palace from the Cave of the Goddess. Both Pramila and Shyamila, each in her way, had wanted to know why they had been disinherited. At first the Matriarch had only been amused. She had pointed out to them that the Question of the Succession was, after all, only an administrative matter. They had then wanted to know why this mere, minor, administrative detail had not been settled in their favour. 'Am I less your daughter than any of the others?' Shyamila had asked, and Pramila had said, 'Doesn't poetry matter?' Gagri the Good hadn't said anything, but she had been more demanding than usual.

'Be quiet,' the Matriarch had commanded. 'The matter is settled. My daughter, Saraswati, shall be my successor, and after her the succession passes to my granddaughter, Gagri the Good.'

But at this Saraswati had demurred. 'Would it not be enough

just to settle the matter of your successor?' She had, after all, to consider the interests of her own daughter. Shyamila and Pramila had seized on this at once.

'Gagri the Good as the eldest daughter of the eldest daughter is the rightful heir,' Shyamila declared. 'Let her be appointed your Successor and I will serve as her regent. But as for Saraswati, she was adopted by Malini Devi and isn't even our sister.'

'You are all equally my daughters,' the Matriarch had told them wearily; but Pramila and Shyamila had remained unconvinced and could not understand why Saraswati had been chosen.

'In what way is she better qualified?' Shyamila had demanded.

'She is less your daughter than I am,' Pramila had added.

In the end the Matriarch had told them to pull themselves together and behave like grown-ups, then she had dismissed them. The following morning she was arrested. The Guild of the Servants of the Goddess in conjunction with the Therapists' Guild and the Poets' Guild had informed the mothers of Maya that the Matriarch, together with her entourage, had taken herself off to the Forest of Retirement. Shyamila the Civil and Sarla Devi would jointly take care of the administration of Maya in her absence.

And so the matter rested. The Blue Donkey glanced at the Matriarch. It was hard to read the Matriarch's mood. She did not appear unduly worried. Was she hurt? Depressed? And hiding it all? She had seated herself under a large banyan. She looked tired, but not discontent. That Saraswati was angered by the loss of the matriarchy and anxious about the welfare of her daughter was obvious. She walked up and down while her mind worked furiously at a plan of campaign. Jyanvi kept in step with her and tried to help. The Blue Donkey settled down beside the Matriarch. They sat in silence. After a while the Matriarch asked, 'Well, is your prophecy fulfilled? Are the Mothers of Maya only daughters and no longer mothers?'

'Not especially, Your Majesty,' replied the Blue Donkey. 'The daughters of Maya are only trying to look after their own interests and the interests of their daughters.'

'I am no longer "Your Majesty",' returned the Matriarch. 'One can't be a matriarch without a matriarchy. This is a forest and in a forest every creature is only itself. You are a donkey and I am an old woman.'

'All right,' agreed the donkey. 'But what happens next?'

'I think Shyamila will send a deputation,' the Matriarch replied.

'And then what will you do?' the Blue Donkey asked.

'I don't know.' The Ranisaheb of Maya smiled at the Blue Donkey companionably. 'I quite like this forest.'

'But if you don't tell them what to do, what will they do?' the Blue Donkey persisted.

Just then Shyamila the Civil and Pramila the Poet, accompanied by several of their followers, burst into the clearing. The followers were armed. Sarla Devi was not among them.

'Well, Mother? Have you reconsidered?' Shyamila the Civil began boldly.

The Matriarch glanced up. 'Reconsidered what?'

Shyamila the Civil looked at her mother. It was extraordinary how the Matriarch had managed to make her seat under the banyan seem like a throne, and the banyan itself like a great canopy protecting her. It made Shyamila feel that she, Shyamila, was a mere petitioner, or, at best, a naughty little girl. She reminded herself that, after all, she had the upper hand. She pulled herself together and answered evenly, 'Have you reconsidered the matter of the succession. I am more your daughter than any of these others. It's only fitting that I should be the next Matriarch.'

But to this the Matriarch responded with an almost imperceptible lift of the eyebrows. 'In what way are you more my daughter?'

'I am most like you,' Shyamila replied with firm conviction. 'I have your strength and your intelligence.'

Pramila the Poet stepped forward. 'But I have your love of poetry,' she put in. 'And that matters most.'

The Matriarch's glance travelled slowly from daughter to daughter. It rested on Saraswati. 'And what about you?' she asked. 'What is your claim to being more my daughter than any of these others?'

Saraswati hesitated. What should she say? To say that she had no claim at all would be foolish. 'Like you, and unlike them, I have borne a daughter,' she answered.

The Matriarch sighed. 'So you feel that whichever one of you is most like me should rule in my stead?'

'Well – ' Pramila started to say.

Shyamila silenced her, 'Be quiet, Pramila.' She confronted the Matriarch. 'Yes, Mother. That's what we think.'

The Matriarch turned to the Blue Donkey. 'The sight of my grown-up daughters behaving like children discourages me. Say something sensible. Explain to them why they ought not to behave like children.'

The Blue Donkey considered. 'Well,' she said soberly, 'I will tell them a story.'

She cleared her throat and began:

'Several hundred miles from Maya, in the middle of the ocean, there was once an island where it was the general practice for the women of the island to eat one another. It was not that they were cruel or unusually savage or even suffering from a shortage of food, it was just that their digestive tract had a peculiarity which enabled them to acquire the essential virtue of any creature they happened to ingest. It followed then that the more evolved the creature, the greater the benefits derived from it. And it was for this reason that the women of this island began eating each other.

When they first made this discovery, murder became such a commonplace occurrence that the population of the island began to decline. Their Matriarch, who was, of course, a prime target, did her best to put a stop to it. Everyone agreed that the mandatory penalty for attempted murder and for murder itself should be death, but a controversy raged about what to do with the resulting bodies. There was a general consensus that the body of the victim should be chopped up carefully and distributed fairly among the populace; but there was some disagreement about what was fair. Some women argued that the children of the victim should be given the lion's share; but others pointed out that the possibility of a gain as large as that was only putting temptation in the way.

Discussion concerning the murderer's body was more ferocious. One group said that the real issue was whether to waste or not to waste. Others argued that to eat the murderer would inevitably make the murderer a part of themselves and that this would be improper. In a sense, it would make the murderer immortal, and vice ought not to be rewarded. It was decided in the end that each woman should be allowed to choose for herself.

Since life was still dangerous, all the islanders made out wills bequeathing their bodies either to their children or to the state, and, in some instances, to their lovers and friends. As for the bodies of the murderers, they were chopped up and placed in the marketplace. Those who wished to were able to partake, but to be seen doing so resulted in disgrace. As a result, though there was a small black market in the bodies of murderers, most of the remains were thrown away. Gulls and vultures and scavenging animals fed on these remains, and in time these creatures acquired the skill and cunning of the women they had eaten. No woman was safe from marauding gulls, no gull was safe from the attack of vultures. Soon a general massacre prevailed. Every creature was eating every other as fast and as furiously as it possibly could. And that was how it happened that life on this island destroyed itself.'

The Blue Donkey paused, and surveyed the women assembled there to see what effect her story had had.

'No, that isn't logical,' the Matriarch commented. 'In the end there ought to have been one creature left. Which one was that?'

'Everyone and no one,' the Blue Donkey replied. 'It's true that in the end there was one glob left, but the essential virtues of all these creatures so warred within its mass that it died before it was born of self-hatred.'

The Ranisaheb nodded. 'Yes, that will do. It satisfies,' she said.

But Jyanvi protested. 'Weren't there any among these creatures who were kind and gentle, so that when they were eaten the Eater was changed?'

'There was one,' the Blue Donkey responded gravely, 'but faced with the terrible choice between being Eater or Eaten, she jumped into a well right at the outset. It's true that the fish in the well ate bits of her body, but this so changed them that they were no longer able to feed themselves. The well acquired a bad reputation and was known to the creatures as the Well of Death.'

At this point Shyamila the Civil interrupted angrily, 'All this is mere verbiage! Tall tales and poetry make nothing happen. Are you or aren't you going to change your mind?'

'I am not going to change my mind.' The Matriarch sounded weary.

'But Mother,' Shyamila burst out in exasperation, 'what difference does it make which of your daughters rules in your stead?'

Suddenly the Matriarch smiled. 'Perhaps you're right,' she said.

'Then you agree to name me as your successor?' Shyamila could not keep the eagerness out of her voice.

'No.'

Shyamila frowned. Why was the Matriarch being so unreasonable? Couldn't she see that agreeing to their demands was mere common sense? 'Mother,' Shyamila tried to be patient, 'can't you see that you have nothing at all to bargain with? The effective power is in our hands. In making any concessions at all, I'm being generous where you're helpless! I came in spite of Sarla's objections. She warned me you'd be obstinate.'

The Matriarch glanced at her daughter. 'You are tedious,' was all she said.

For a moment Shyamila the Civil wanted to stamp her foot, and yell with frustration; but she managed to make herself answer quietly, 'With due respect, so are you, Mother.' She summoned her followers and left.

10

But she was a heretic

'Don't you see? It's absolutely essential that we march into Maya, depose Shyamila and get the matriarchy back.' Saraswati was exasperated. What was self-evident to her seemed to be less than obvious to Jyanvi and the Blue Donkey. But then they were foreigners. It was the Ranisaheb's reactions that had baffled her completely. After all that had happened, that her own mother should appear so indifferent made no sense at all. The Matriarch was lying down in a crude shelter of leafy branches which the others had made for her. She had said that the events of the past two days had tired her. It was Jyanvi and the Blue Donkey whom Saraswati was addressing. She went on, 'I don't understand my mother at all. It isn't like her to be so resigned. Is she simply going to let Shyamila have her own way?'

It was on the tip of Jyanvi's tongue to say, 'Yes, why not? What does it matter?' But she managed not to say it.

'Perhaps the Matriarch is upset by the spectacle of her daughters quarrelling among themselves,' the Blue Donkey suggested.

'Perhaps,' replied Saraswati, 'but I can't let the matter rest. Will you help me?' It was a direct request.

Jyanvi and the Blue Donkey did not answer immediately. Which of the Matriarch's daughters ruled didn't really matter to them. Or did it matter? Jyanvi had begun to think that life in the forest had distinct advantages. She would probably be able to think in peace. She would have Saraswati all to herself, and both Gagri and Sona would be far away and being looked after by somebody else... However, Jyanvi also realised that this was not a point of view Saraswati would share. Why start an argument she was unlikely to win and which could only offend? She said, yes, of course she would help. The Blue Donkey's stance was more disinterested, but she liked Saraswati. 'Yes. All right,' she agreed. 'But it depends on the Matriarch,' she added.

'Oh, the Matriarch will come round. She's just tired. Now,' Saraswati continued briskly, 'what we need is a plan of action. What do you suggest?'

Jyanvi thought fast. She wanted at least to be thought to be trying to do her best. 'Let's see if we can find Asha the Apostate and ask for her help.'

'Who?' Saraswati was startled.

'Asha the Apostate,' Jyanvi repeated. 'She was exiled to this forest, wasn't she?'

'But she was a heretic!'

Saraswati had been taken aback by Jyanvi's suggestion, but the Blue Donkey murmured quietly, 'Does it matter now? Under the circumstances?'

As Saraswati was considering this, they found themselves surrounded by fifteen young men. Each of them carried a short, wooden rod. 'We would like you to accompany us,' said the leader gravely.

Saraswati was completely outraged. 'Since when do pretty boys make requests?'

But in response the fifteen young men only looked puzzled. The Blue Donkey looked at them carefully. They were only boys, and they were pretty in their light kurtas and bright sarongs. She noticed that the rods they were carrying were elaborately carved. Were they toys or weapons? Two or three of the boys had wooden dolls. Perhaps they were playing a game? 'What happens if we refuse?' she enquired, trying to enter into the spirit of it.

'Then we must go back and ask for instructions,' answered one of them.

The noise had woken up the Matriarch. At first she thought that the group of pretty boys was part of a dream, but she had heard their interchange with the Blue Donkey. Even if it was a dream, she had better see it through. 'Who sent you?' she asked them.

'Our mother,' replied the leader of the fifteen.

'And who is your "mother"?' demanded the Matriarch.

'Our mother is the Princess Asha. She was exiled from Maya for saving our lives.'

The young man had said this in all seriousness. The Matriarch didn't know what to make of it. She found herself asking, 'And do you always do what your mother tells you?'

'Yes!' he replied.

Somehow, in spite of herself, this reminded the Matriarch of Gagri the Good. 'Well,' she told him, 'then go and tell your mother that her mother has summoned her here.'

The fifteen young men gaped at the Matriarch. 'Are you the Matriarch of Maya Nagar, the fabled city?' asked the leader incredulously.

'Yes,' the Matriarch said briskly. 'I'm your mother's mother. Now, do as you're told.'

It was obvious that the boys were having trouble taking it in. It was as though a fabled creature had appeared among them suddenly. They stared at the Matriarch a few seconds longer, then they filed away into the forest and were lost among the green leaves.

Before the others could say anything, the Matriarch informed them that she was still tired and intended to rest. The Blue Donkey settled beside her and dozed off as well. Jyanvi felt uneasy. Anything could happen. They were no longer in a city governed by women. Of course, not that Maya had been altogether safe, but still... Didn't the Matriarch and the Blue Donkey care? Saraswati at least looked suitably worried. Jyanvi wondered whether she was really going to ask for the Apostate's help. And then what would happen? Would they march into

Maya with an army of young men with Asha at their head? Armed with wooden rods? It would be stupid. On the other hand, was staying in the forest really a good idea? She would have liked a bath, but the brook they had found was hardly adequate. And though the berries and fruits they had eaten for dinner had been delicious, still fruit for dinner night after night and only fruit would not be pleasant. There was something to be said for hot meals, comfortable beds...

Jyanvi kept her thoughts to herself and waited. But when the leaves rustled and twigs cracked, it wasn't Asha the Apostate and her troops entering, it was Valerie looking flustered and distressed.

'Hello,' said Jyanvi, 'what are you doing here?'

'Oh, it's you,' responded Valerie. 'Where's the Matriarch? I have a message.' She stumbled towards the Ranisaheb and fell at her feet.

'Your Majesty, the Princess Pramila craves your pardon. So does Malini Devi, the Lesser Matriarch. They asked me to tell you that Gagri the Good and Saraswati's daughter are quite safe. The Guild of Poets and the supporters of Malini Devi are at your disposal. They beg you to return from the forest.'

The Matriarch sat up and examined Valerie sleepily. 'Thank you for bringing news of the children. Just why do Pramila and Malini Devi want me to return?'

'They are troubled by the injustice and tyranny of the Princess Shyamila and that of her consort, Sarla Devi, Chief of the Guild of the Servants of the Goddess.' It was a rehearsed speech and Valerie repeated it kneeling before the Matriarch.

'Yes, I understand the rhetoric,' the Matriarch told her. 'Now get up and give me a proper explanation.'

Valerie got to her feet slowly. 'Well, the thing is, Your Majesty,' she said awkwardly, 'they're going to disband the Guild of Poets – merge it perhaps with the Goddess' Servants. According to them, poets are useful, but they shouldn't be autonomous. The Princess Pramila is very upset.'

Jyanvi suppressed a grin and kept quiet. The Matriarch was

questioning Valerie further. 'And why is the Lesser Matriarch troubled?'

'The Princess Shyamila has ruled that that particular house has no legitimate heir after Malini Devi and that all their privileges and properties revert.'

'Revert to whom?' demanded the Matriarch.

'To the Matriarchate, which in turn, it is rumoured, intends to hand them over to the Chief of the Goddess' Servants. That would make Sarla Devi a Lesser Matriarch and that in turn – '

Before Valerie could explain further, they were interrupted by the sound of conch shells. The fifteen young men, now accompanied by many others, marched into the clearing, divided into two rows, came to a halt and waited, while a dozen other young men brought in a palanquin upon their shoulders. Then they all fell on their knees, bowed their heads, flourished their rods and cried out loudly, 'The Empress Asha! The Empress Asha is here!'

A middle-aged woman climbed out carefully. She wore a white sari with a purple border, which had been washed and ironed, but looked old. She had a pleasant face. She bowed slightly to the Matriarch. 'Well, Mother?'

'Well, daughter? What is the meaning of this?' The Matriarch indicated the bowed heads.

Asha the Apostate smiled. She appeared unembarrassed. 'Oh,' she said, 'the boys like it. It's only a game. They say it gives them a sense of cohesion. Would you like me to send them away? Or will you come with us to where we live so that we can make you more comfortable?'

'We will come,' the Matriarch replied.

'Wait, Mother!' Saraswati interrupted. 'Oughtn't we to find out a little more? Discuss matters further?'

Asha the Apostate turned to Saraswati. 'You must be Saraswati. You were only a little girl when I last saw you. Welcome to the forest.'

Saraswati looked at her eldest sister doubtfully. She pulled herself together. 'Thank you,' she said. 'May I present Jyanvi and the Blue Donkey? And this is Valerie. Perhaps you remember her?'

'How do you do?' Asha the Apostate greeted each one of them in the friendliest possible way. 'Will you accompany us?' she asked politely.

The Blue Donkey agreed with alacrity. She was most interested, and besides, she found Asha the Apostate congenial. The others felt uncertain. But what were they to do? They accepted the invitation with more or less grace.

11

A loyal Mayan

Ashagad, or the Fortress of Hope, was some distance away. Once they left the forest, the terrain became hilly and barren. Black stones were scattered about and on some of the rocks it was still possible to see the concentric rings which the lava had made. High overhead the sun blazed and hawks circled on the thermal currents. The Ranisaheb was enjoying herself. She looked about her with great interest. After a while she tired, and then the pretty boys carried her in the palanquin. Saraswati had her doubts about whether any of it was at all proper or indeed advisable, but for the moment there seemed to be little choice.

At last, after a steep climb, they reached the stronghold. Even Saraswati was impressed. The inhabitants of Ashagad were cliff-dwellers. They had cut splendid chambers in the cliff face to house themselves. Below them lay their fields and the broad stream which irrigated them. The general effect was neither impoverished, nor uncivilised. Jyanvi and the Blue Donkey were reminded of the Cave Temple, though these chambers had been constructed much more recently and there were only a few carvings here and there. The carvings appeared to celebrate the Empress, or perhaps it was the goddess, but unlike the carvings in the Cave Temple the female figure was usually surrounded by a group of young men, and just occasionally by a little boy and a little girl. Valerie wondered what the Mayans made of it, but neither the Matriarch nor Saraswati offered any comment.

After the visitors had bathed and refreshed themselves, they were invited to dine with Asha. Would it please them, the Apostate enquired, to be entertained first with a dance recital? 'Yes,' the Matriarch replied, 'that would be most agreeable.'

They found, to their surprise, that the dancing was good and the music excellent, it was just the story that was a little obscure. The principal dancers consisted of a tree and two young men. The two young men seemed to be imploring the tree to give them something. The dancer who played the tree expressed the tree's indifference by the most minute and subtle of gestures. Then, towards the end, when the two young men had almost given up, the tree relented and appeared to shed a blessing on them.

'Beautifully done,' the Mayans murmured and over dinner congratulated Asha on the skill of the dancers.

Asha the Apostate turned eagerly to her mother, 'Now will you admit that boys can be civilised?'

The Matriarch looked up in surprise, 'My dear, whether or not they can be civilised was never in dispute. It's just that it was never considered particularly worthwhile.'

For a fraction of a second Asha the Apostate looked as though her mother had slapped her, but she said lightly, 'Well, we won't argue now. Tomorrow I'd like you to meet Mohan and Madhu. Perhaps they'll convince you better than I can.'

'Who are Mohan and Madhu?' enquired the Matriarch.

'My eldest boys.' Was there a touch of defiance in Asha's manner?

'You call them yours?' Saraswati had been startled into speaking before she could stop herself.

'Yes, I call them mine.' Open hostility had replaced the defiance.

Before any further damage was done, the Blue Donkey said quickly, 'I greatly enjoyed the dance performance, but I'm not sure I understood it. I wonder if you could explain something to me please?'

'Certainly.' Asha the Apostate smiled. She sensed an ally in the Blue Donkey though she could not have explained why.

'Well.' The Blue Donkey collected her thoughts. 'Who were the two young men, and why were they beseeching the tree?'

'The two young men were mothers and they were beseeching the tree to grant them a child,' Asha replied.

'But how could they be mothers?' It was Valerie who protested this time.

However, Asha the Apostate had regained her composure. 'The institutions of Ashagad are not unlike those of Maya Nagar,' she explained politely. 'Those young men had passed all the tests and attained adult status.'

'But why did they pray to a tree?' asked Jyanvi, feeling that this, at least, was a harmless question.

'In Ashagad, when a youngster passes his first test, he carves himself a wooden doll,' Asha told her. 'It symbolises the baby which he hopes to receive from the Tree of Life. Many of the youngsters also carve short, wooden rods, which represent the Tree itself.'

'A charming myth,' Jyanvi murmured.

'Oh, it's not a myth,' Asha replied. 'There's a tree in the forest underneath which we find boy babies. Ask the Matriarch. I'm sure the mothers of Maya know of it. We call it the Tree of Life.'

For the first time in their acquaintance, Jyanvi saw the Matriarch flinch, but the old woman's voice was steady enough when she answered. 'Yes, there is such a tree. We call it the Tree of Death.'

Jyanvi and the Blue Donkey were appalled. They had hoped to smooth over differences, not uncover infanticide.

For a moment, no one knew what to say. Fortunately dinner was served. They were waited upon by two or three of Asha's young men. The visitors commented upon the food, finding it delicious. The chapatis were hot and properly layered. The vegetables were fresh and suitably spiced. As they ate they felt better tempered, and for a while it seemed likely that good humour would prevail. But Saraswati had decided that there was nothing to be gained by being circumspect. 'Please,' she said, 'I do not in the least wish to offend, only to understand. Are you the only real mother here?'

Asha the Apostate looked at her coldly. 'Of course not. However, to answer you accurately in Mayan terms, terms which I hope you will understand, I am the only Grade B mother here.'

'And you have borne children?' Saraswati continued. Jyanvi and the Blue Donkey glanced at her. What had got into Saraswati? Didn't she appreciate that she was a foreigner here?

Asha the Apostate replied with cold fury. 'I have borne one daughter. When she was still a baby she was taken away from me.'

The Matriarch put an arm around Asha. 'Gagri is well,' she told her softly. 'Saraswati is a Mayan, after all. Try to be patient with her. She means no harm.'

The Blue Donkey intervened again. 'Gagri the Good is a delightful child,' she said to Asha gently. 'Forgive us for being so clumsy. I think the question that is exercising all of us is how you maintain your population.'

Asha the Apostate looked at her in surprise. 'Surely that's obvious? By stealing from the mothers of Maya, of course.'

But Saraswati was amazed. 'Do you mean to say you've stolen our children and the matter has gone unnoticed?'

It was Saraswati whom the Matriarch restrained this time. 'No dear, Asha doesn't mean that they've stolen the daughters of Maya. She is referring to the pretty boys.'

'That's right,' Asha told them calmly. 'We steal the pretty boys, the ones who are left under the Tree whenever there's a surplus.'

'But why?' Saraswati asked. None of it made any sense to her. 'What are they good for? They're warlike and sterile. And they can't even reproduce themselves. What's the point?'

'It's the mothers of Maya who produce them,' Asha pointed out, doing her best to be patient with Saraswati.

'But that's only for the semen,' Saraswati replied.

Asha the Apostate looked at her sister in exasperation. 'Look.

Would you kill one of the daughters of Maya or leave her under the Tree to die?'

'Of course not.'

'Then why are you willing to destroy the pretty boys?' Asha thought that perhaps now Saraswati would see the point.

But Saraswati only shook her head. 'It's not the same thing at all,' she said. 'And in any case we don't want to kill them. It's simply a matter of keeping down numbers.'

Asha the Apostate gave up then. 'I see,' she said quietly, 'that during my years of exile very little has changed in Maya.'

'Ah, but there has been a terrible upheaval only recently,' Valerie chimed in. 'Your sister, Shyamila, has usurped the throne.'

Asha laughed. 'Who'd have thought that Shyamila had it in her!' She found it hard to take it seriously.

'Sarla Devi egged her on,' Saraswati explained. 'We've all been exiled.'

Asha realised that for the others it was a very serious matter indeed. 'Is this true?' Asha looked to her mother for an explanation, but, receiving none, contented herself with saying, 'This is indeed a surprising turn of events.'

'And it must be rectified,' Saraswati was persistent. 'Will you help us?'

'Help you do what?' Asha asked.

'Regain the Matriarchate of Maya,' Saraswati said promptly.

Asha the Apostate smiled. 'How and why would I help you to do that?'

'With the help of the pretty boys we might succeed,' Saraswati replied. 'As for why you should help us, that depends on you. Perhaps we can give you something in return? A free pardon? The chance to be a Mayan again? Something like that.'

At this Asha the Apostate laughed openly. 'Now Saraswati, do consider, are you, a loyal Mayan, seriously proposing that we march upon Maya with an army of pretty boys?'

Saraswati had the grace to look embarrassed. 'Well. We needn't actually march upon the city. A threat might be enough.' She glanced at Valerie. 'We have received offers of help.'

'I see.' Asha the Apostate still looked amused. 'And once my pretty boys have helped you regain Maya Nagar, what will you do for them?'

'What would you like?' Saraswati countered.

'A change in the institutions of Maya and equal rights for boys,' Asha said in a strong voice. 'Boys should also be given a decent education and be allowed to grow up into mothers like everyone else.'

'But they're not capable!' Saraswati protested.

'The pretty boys can't become biological mothers, but they're certainly capable of Grade A and Grade C status. We've proved it here in Ashagad.' Asha kept her voice as reasonable as possible.

'Well, that may be as it may be.' Saraswati looked sceptical. She knew that her eldest sister had odd ideas. After all, that was why she had been exiled. 'If I may say so,' she said deliberately, 'the internal workings of the Mayan matriarchy have absolutely nothing to do with you.'

Asha the Apostate was still smiling. 'Very well. Then what about a trade agreement between the Matriarchate of Maya and the Fortress of Asha in return for our help?'

'A trade agreement?' Asha's proposal had taken Saraswati by surprise. 'But what do you want? Oh yes, of course . . .'

'That's right,' Asha told her. 'What we want is the Mayan surplus of males. Indeed, why not let us have all of them? In return we'd supply you with semen.'

Saraswati frowned. 'But that wouldn't be good sense, since we can already provide for our own supply with very little trouble and expense.'

The Matriarch put a stop to this interchange. 'Asha is having a game with you,' she told Saraswati. 'You're a good Mayan and well brought up, but you're also completely out of your depth. Be quiet.'

It was a snub, but the Matriarch had judged it necessary. She now turned to her other daughter. 'You're older than Saraswati. Stop teasing her. And be serious.'

'But, Mother,' Asha the Apostate smiled at the Matriarch, 'I was being serious. Indeed, I've now thought of a better plan. We could exchange some of the daughters of Maya for the sons of Ashagad.' Saraswati had annoyed Asha thoroughly and Asha could not resist baiting her.

'What do you mean?' Saraswati interrupted. 'In exchange for us, demand a supply of boys from the Mayans? Haven't you understood? Shyamila has exiled us. She doesn't want us back.'

'You've misunderstood,' Asha replied. 'I meant the straightforward exchange of boys for girls.'

'Never!' Saraswati was on her feet with outrage.

'Be quiet, both of you!' The Matriarch silenced both her daughters.

'Yes, Mother.' Asha the Apostate answered meekly enough, and Saraswati sat down again, but the Matriarch knew that there was a limit to the obedience she could exact from them. She leaned heavily on the Blue Donkey that night as they made their way along the stone corridors.

As for the others, Valerie didn't know whether to be pleased or puzzled; Saraswati was in a bad mood; and Jyanvi, as was becoming increasingly normal for her, was merely anxious.

She had a dream that night. The Blue Donkey was ensconced on a throne carved out of the mountainside. Before her were assembled all the creatures, and behind her the mothers of Maya had grouped themselves. In the foreground, immediately below her, were dozens and dozens of mewling babies. Jyanvi herself wasn't in the dream, and for this she felt grateful. Suddenly a great voice – perhaps it was the goddess – roared out the question: 'Shall these creatures live?' The Blue Donkey looked up in astonishment. 'Yes', she replied. 'Why not? All creatures want to live.' She seemed not to have understood the significance of the question, much less its moral dimension. She got to her feet and ambled away along the slope to nibble some grass.

Jyanvi wondered whether to tell the Blue Donkey about her dream, then decided better not.

12

Ashan babies

Mohan and Madhu were charming — by any standards. Privately Saraswati conceded that. They were well mannered, eager to please, and they deferred to her most gratifyingly. In their own way they were probably even quite good looking. They had been delegated by Asha to look after the visitors. Asha herself was in conference with the Matriarch and the Blue Donkey. Saraswati had felt a little put out that she too had not been invited to confer, but had decided to make the best of it. After all, Jyanvi and Valerie were with her. They were drinking tea by the great pool which supplied Ashagad with water. The greenness of the pool, the lotus leaves, the small fish darting about, the shady trees and the pleasant patchwork of red earth and green fields in the valley below would have made it difficult for anyone to remain bad tempered.

Mohan was answering a question Jyanvi had just asked. 'The group of three that you see over and over again in the carvings are Kurup and Kripa, the first children, and their mother, the goddess.'

'But in most of the carvings I've seen, their mother seems to be angry with them. Why is that?'

Madhu smiled at Jyanvi. 'Well, you know how it is. We make up stories to explain ourselves. The goddess is angry with the boy, Kurup, because he doesn't look like her and won't grow up into a proper woman. And because she isn't altogether certain whether she wants him or not, she sends him away. That's why he's crying.'

'What about the little girl?' Jyanvi wanted to know. 'Why is the goddess angry with her?'

'Because she laughed at Kurup, and said he was useless and would never be able to be a mother at all,' Madhu replied.

Saraswati had been trying to follow the conversation, but Madhu's last remark puzzled her. After all, the little girl had only told the truth. 'But why did that make the goddess angry?' she asked.

Madhu, in turn, looked puzzled. To him the answer was self-evident. He did his best, however. 'Well, because the goddess had made Kurup, after all.'

Jyanvi decided that this was dangerous ground; and besides, she wanted to know the rest of the story. 'And then what happened?' she prompted.

'Then the goddess cursed the little girl and said that without Kurup's help, she, Kripa, would also be barren. That's why she's crying,' Madhu explained.

'I see. Thank you for telling us.' Jyanvi did not comment on the story. She glanced at Saraswati, but Saraswati was also being discreet. It was Valerie who burst out, 'You know, I originally came from a country where the pretty boys rule.'

'Ah, yes,' Mohan said pleasantly, 'your country must have been like Ashagad. Were you their Empress? And what did they do after you left?'

'They didn't even notice that I'd left,' Valerie told him. 'You don't understand. My country was crowded with many other women, just like me. One more or less didn't really matter.'

Mohan looked surprised. 'But mothers always matter,' he said reasonably. 'If there were many other mothers like you, then how can you say that the "pretty boys" ruled? By the way, we'd prefer it if you didn't use that expression. We call ourselves Ashans.'

'Sorry,' Valerie acknowledged the correction. 'It's hard to explain,' she went on. 'You see the "Ashans" and the "Mayans" in my country all lived together. And the "Ashans" bullied the "Mayans".'

'I see.' Mohan was doing his best to be polite, though it was obvious he thought privately that Valerie was probably talking a great deal of nonsense. 'It would be an unusual arrangement, wouldn't it? Why did the Ashans bully the Mayans? In what way?'

Valerie looked at Jyanvi for help, but Jyanvi was staring determinedly at the pool. As for Saraswati, she looked as mystified as the Ashans. Valerie struggled on bravely. 'Well, you see, the Ashans wanted the Mayans to bear their children.'

'Well, obviously only a Mayan can be a biological mother, an Ashan can't. Is that what you mean?' Mohan was frowning with the effort to understand.

'No, I mean that the Ashans enslaved the Mayans and divided them up among themselves. The more important the Ashan, the more Mayans he owned.' Valerie spaced out the words in the hope that if she said everything slowly it would all become clear.

Now Madhu was frowning. 'But for what purpose would Ashans wish to enslave Mayans? And besides, how could they? Why didn't the Mayans stop them?'

Valerie was beginning to wish she had kept quiet, but the young men were looking at her expectantly. She took a deep breath. 'Well, you see, only the Ashans existed, the Mayans did not exist.'

'But you just said —'

'I mean that only the Ashans really mattered,' Valerie clarified.

'Do you mean that only the Ashans mattered to the Ashans and only the Mayans mattered to the Mayans?' Madhu asked.

'Not exactly. I mean that the Ashans had all the power. No, don't interrupt. Think of it this way. Every Ashan thought of himself as a kind of farmer, and of every Mayan as a bit of land or a field which could be his property.'

'What?' Some of Valerie's ideas seemed so outlandish that the two Ashans were having trouble believing their ears.

'His property,' Valerie repeated, 'which could be used for growing babies. Now do you see?'

Madhu shook his head apologetically, but Mohan's face suddenly lit up. 'I think I can explain,' he told Madhu eagerly. 'I think she means that in her country the Ashans find their babies in the fields rather than under a tree as we do here.' He had managed to make sense out of Valerie's story, and looked pleased with himself.

Jyanvi suppressed a grin, but Valerie noticed it. 'You might have helped,' she said reproachfully.

'Helped to do what?' Jyanvi responded.

'Explain matters.'

'Why?'

Valerie gave up. She turned to the Ashans conversationally. 'Have you any babies?' she asked.

Madhu smiled. A fond expression crossed his face. 'We have both achieved Grade A status. I have a little boy. Mohan is still waiting for his baby.'

'When will he get one?' Jyanvi enquired, feeling she ought to make some contribution, particularly since Saraswati was saying almost nothing at all.

'Soon, I think,' Mohan replied. 'As soon as the Tree proves kind.'

'Are babies plentiful?'

'Oh, no.'

But at this point Saraswati put in a question. 'Are the babies you find always pretty boys – I mean, little Ashans?'

'Yes, of course,' Mohan replied.

'What would you do if you found a Mayan baby?' Jyanvi couldn't resist asking.

Mohan and Madhu hesitated. That possibility had never occurred to them. 'Give her back to the Mayans, I suppose,' said Mohan at last. 'What would we do with her? Mayans and Ashans don't mix.' He nodded politely in Valerie's direction. 'I mean, at least for us it's not customary.'

'But you have an Empress,' Valerie pointed out.

'Yes, but she's the First Mother, the representative of the goddess, and there's only one of her,' Mohan replied.

'I suppose we could keep the little Mayan as a sort of Empress-in-training,' Madhu ventured with a smile.

The Ashans offered them more tea and samosas. The visitors accepted gratefully. Saraswati was just about to make some comment about their system of irrigation, when Valerie, who had suddenly seen a way of making the Ashans understand what she had been saying, demanded abruptly, 'What would you do if the supply of babies ceased?'

Mohan put down the plate of samosas he had been handing around. 'Well, I suppose we'd ask the Mayans to give us some, please. That's where they originally come from, don't they?'

'What if the mothers of Maya refused?' Valerie persisted.

The Ashans thought about it. 'We could offer to pay them for the babies supplied,' Mohan offered.

'But what if the mothers of Maya said there wasn't anything you could pay them with?' There was an intensity in Valerie's manner that would not be denied.

'Then I suppose we'd have to make them,' Madhu replied reluctantly.

'How?'

Valerie was looking straight at him. 'By using force, I suppose,' Madhu mumbled. He looked away, he didn't like any of it.

But Valerie had got what she wanted. 'Now do you see?' she cried triumphantly.

'See what?' Mohan asked. He tried to keep the annoyance out of his voice. What was this stranger going on about?

'Why the Ashans in my country have enslaved the Mayans,' Valerie replied.

Mohan shook his head. What did that have to do with anything? 'No, I don't see.'

'But don't you understand? They've enslaved them in order to force them to have their babies.' For a moment Valerie wondered if the Ashans were being wilfully stupid.

Mohan was startled. 'Ashan babies?'

'No, Ashan and Mayan babies who then belong to a particular Ashan,' Valerie explained.

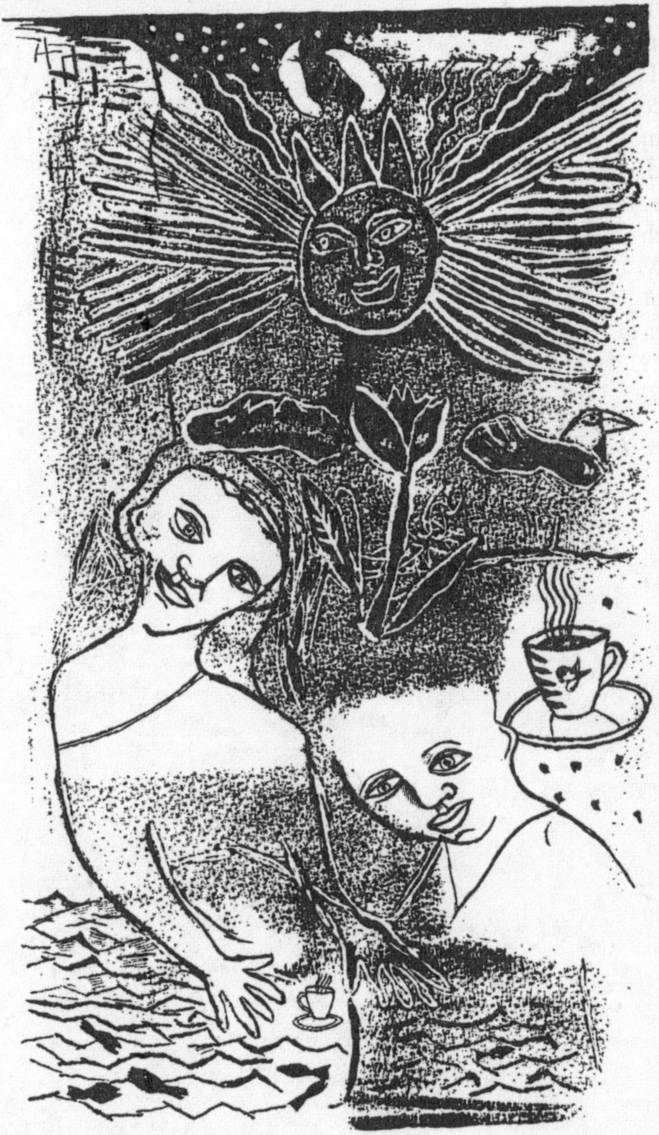

Madhu sighed. It was obvious that Valerie was not going to let up. She would have to be humoured. 'In what way?' he asked politely.

'The babies are branded by his specific genes,' Valerie told them.

Both Mohan and Madhu protested. 'How can that be?'

Valerie explained. 'Because only his semen is used to impregnate the Mayan who belongs to him.' Mohan and Madhu were already looking a little sick so she omitted the details, but she concluded by saying, 'So you see why the exclusive ownership of a Mayan is so important to an Ashan in my society.'

'With due respect,' Madhu murmured, 'none of it sounds at all pleasing.'

'It isn't,' Valerie replied.

'But who then is the mother of the baby?' Mohan asked.

Valerie thought about it. 'An Ashan is always the Grade A mother, and a Mayan is always the Grade B mother,' she said at last, 'but the Ashan delegates his duties to the Mayan. Sometimes, if they're rich, they hire a number of Mayans and very occasionally an Ashan or two to function as Grade C's.'

'I see,' said Mohan. He had had enough. He rose to his feet. 'Thank you for explaining all this to us. It was very interesting. Now, would you like to see our fields?'

'Yes, please,' Jyanvi and Saraswati replied instantly. Saraswati had been getting increasingly bored, and was glad of the relief. But Valerie felt upset though she tried to hide it. It seemed to her that Saraswati and the Ashans looked down on her for having come from a mixed society. And as for Jyanvi, presumably she thought that, as a lesbian, she wasn't implicated in any of it.

Valerie walked away a little ahead of the others, but Madhu sensed her mood. 'Come,' he said. 'We have lunch prepared for you by one of the canals in the valley below. It's pleasant there. We'll roast fresh grain. I think you'll like it. Let's enjoy ourselves.' He linked arms with her. Valerie sighed. She had forgotten how many years it was since she had walked arm in arm with a handsome young male; but to this young one she was, she supposed, no more than a friendly creature from another species. Well, it was, as Mohan had said, all very interesting. She felt lonely.

13

Loathsome reptile

Asha the Apostate entered Madhu's chambers. They were sparsely furnished and beautifully proportioned. Some of the furniture had been cut from the stone and on the right hand wall was a carving, as yet unfinished, of an enormous neem tree. Each one of the leaves was carefully delineated, right down to the serrated edges. Asha glanced at it and smiled at Madhu. 'It's coming along nicely. Mohan must be pleased with it. Have you a moment to spare?'

Madhu smiled back. 'Yes, Mother, but we'll have to be quiet. I've just managed to make Balu sleep. I don't want him to wake up and start crying again.'

He rose to his feet and carried the baby to its little cot and tucked it in. The baby continued to sleep peacefully. For a moment they stood side by side and watched the sleeping baby.

'It's his teeth, of course,' Asha murmured. 'Is he all right otherwise?'

Madhu nodded. 'I think so. He's been a bit cranky.'

Asha patted Madhu's shoulder. 'You look tired.'

Madhu smiled. 'I am a little. Balu cried through most of the night. I wish we lived somewhere where there were more trained mothers.' He waited for his mother to sit, then sat down wearily.

Asha looked at him sitting there in his blue sarong and white kurta. Whatever the mothers of Maya thought, he was clever and graceful. And he was beautiful. She was proud of him. 'Would you like to live in Maya Nagar?' she asked him.

Madhu hesitated, 'If you'd asked me yesterday, I might have said "Yes", or "I don't know", but now I think not.' He frowned slightly as he thought of the morning's conversation.

'Why?' Asha inquired. 'Did our visitors put you off?' She was only mildly concerned.

'No, not exactly,' Madhu replied. 'They were perfectly pleasant. It's just that one of them described a society in which Ashans and Mayans lived together. It was horrible!' Madhu grimaced. 'She talked about slavery and other practices which seem unimaginable.'

Asha smiled at Madhu reassuringly. 'Oh, I didn't mean would you like to live in Maya as one of their "pretty boys". I meant would you like to live in Maya as a fellow Mayan – as their equal?'

'I suppose so,' Madhu sounded doubtful. 'You know, in the society Valerie described, the Mayans were the slaves and we owned them.'

'Who is "we"?' Asha looked at him sharply.

'Ashans, of course. Who else?' Madhu looked surprised.

'I see,' Asha sat up. 'Well, I'm sorry to hear that our guests have been putting such rubbish into your head. Valerie, of course, is an outsider – not a Mayan.'

The disapproval in Asha's voice was evident, but Madhu didn't respond to it. He was trying to formulate a question. At last he said, 'Mother, are you an Ashan or a Mayan?'

It took Asha by surprise. 'What do you mean? I was born in Maya. I grew up in Maya, and I rule in Ashagad. I suppose if you must use these ridiculous labels, then I'm both.'

'But can I be both?' Madhu was frowning with the effort to think the matter through. 'I don't see how I can call myself a Mayan.'

'Well, what if you can't?' Asha replied briskly. 'Let's say you're an Ashan. How does it matter?'

'It would matter if the Ashans and Mayans fought one another,' Madhu said slowly.

Asha stared at him. 'Why would we fight each other? What an extraordinary idea! Only this morning, when we were discussing the possibility of a trade agreement, one of the problems we came up against was that Mayans and Ashans really have very little in common.'

Madhu hesitated, then he said in a troubled voice, 'Mother, everyone knows that the Mayans have something we want – Ashan babies. If the supply dried up, we'd have to fight them.'

Asha felt a tremendous sadness. Was this what it had come to? Still, she had better find out just where these ideas had led Madhu. She tugged at the end of her sari and wrapped it about her shoulders firmly.

'I see. Is this what the Mayans have been telling you?'

'No, not exactly. We were just talking.' Madhu looked at his mother. He tried to explain. 'It's just that I realised clearly, for the first time, that for our supply of babies we are dependent on Mayans.'

Asha leaned across and ruffled Madhu's hair. 'It was you who made up the story of Kripa and Kurup,' she told him gently. 'You're needed as well.'

But Madhu only looked more troubled. 'No, Mother, that's just the point. Ashans aren't needed. The Mayans have their own supply of captive Ashans. They call them the "pretty boys" – Peebies. You know that.' He paused and added hesitantly, 'Mother, what if we had our own supply of captive Mayans to make our Ashan babies for us? Then we wouldn't be dependent on them.'

Asha recoiled in anger. 'I'm ashamed of you. I didn't know you were capable of such a disgusting idea!'

Madhu apologised. 'I didn't really mean it. I was only trying to work things out. Besides, it's not my own idea. It's Valerie's.'

'Valerie's?'

'Well, Valerie said that where she came from, the Ashans owned the Mayans and made them make babies for them,' he told Asha.

Asha didn't know what to make of this. 'Did she explain why?' she asked Madhu.

'No, but when Mohan and I discussed it with the others, Mohan suggested that if it were really true that the Ashans and Mayans lived together, then it would be the only way to make the Mayans bear a lot of Ashans.' He looked at Asha. 'That must be why.'

Asha was beginning to find the whole thing more and more puzzling, but it was important to find out what was going on. 'Why,' she asked carefully, 'would anyone want to force the Mayans to bear more Ashans?'

Madhu looked surprised. 'So that then there would be more of us! Look,' he went on reasonably, 'we worked out that to make babies a large number of Ashans simply aren't needed. And anyway the Mayans would probably want to make more Mayans. They wouldn't be bothered making Ashans.' He glanced involuntarily in the direction of his own child.

Asha frowned. 'I see. So you've been discussing all this among yourselves. Do you realise how much harm you've done!'

Madhu had never seen his mother quite so angry. 'We were only tossing ideas about,' he protested. 'They're only ideas. What harm can they do?'

'And you call yourself a poet!' Madhu winced under the contempt in Asha's voice. She went on more quietly, 'You'd better tell me the rest.'

Madhu looked shamefaced. 'Well,' he blurted out, 'Mohan suggested the idea of "war".'

Asha could hardly believe it. 'Are you saying that Mohan wanted to make war on the Mayans?'

'Oh, no,' Madhu replied. 'He didn't want to do any such thing. It was only an idea, an abstraction. He just wanted to think it through.'

'I see. And may one enquire what his conclusions were?'

It was obvious Asha was very angry, and Madhu almost wished he hadn't said anything; but the ideas disturbed him and he had wanted to know what his mother thought. Well, he might as well carry on. 'It was simply that the logical conclusion was war, Mother. You see, to be absolutely certain of a supply of babies, we'd have to enslave a few Mayans. And to do that we'd have to make war.'

'Well,' Asha replied. 'Since we're being logical, did anyone point out that rather a large number of Mayans would be needed?'

'Yes,' Madhu mumbled.

But Asha went on relentlessly. 'And did anyone further point out that if you made war on the Mayans and killed them, that you'd then be left with a shortage of Mayans and in consequence of babies?'

Madhu was feeling more and more uncomfortable, but he replied truthfully. 'We sent someone off to ask Valerie, but she got angry and upset. We didn't really understand it properly. She seemed to be saying that in order to subdue and humiliate the Mayans, and also in order to make more babies, the Ashans impregnated them.'

'What!'

'Well, it was very muddled. I told you it didn't make sense,' Madhu said wretchedly. 'And anyway there was another idea which several of us found more interesting, and that was being able to stamp your own babies genetically.' He glanced at Balu's cot and continued painfully, 'I love Balu, but if I knew that he carried half my genes, then I think I might feel differently. Perhaps love him more? I don't know. There's something about the idea that is so seductive . . .' He glanced at Asha. 'And at the same time all these ideas are so revolting!' He stopped and looked helpless.

But for once Asha remained unmoved by his misery. 'And so what did you conclude? To make war or not to make war?' she enquired coldly.

'Oh Mother, we concluded nothing. It was simply a matter of logic. You see, we were particularly taken with the idea of having babies of our own, that is, genetically branded babies . . . So if that was the end, then enslaving a few Mayans was the logical means. None of it was serious. We were only kicking ideas around. We meant no harm,' Madhu pleaded.

Asha stood up. 'Nonetheless, you may have done a great

deal of harm. You and Mohan have behaved like a pair of irresponsible children. How could you? You who have the status of a mother? This isn't a game. You're not "kicking ideas around". I'll send someone to look after Balu. Please pull yourself together. Take two guards with you and place Valerie in solitary confinement. Tell her that this is being done for her own protection. Then send Mohan to me. And Madhu –'

'Yes, Mother?'

'Grow up.'

It was late at night. Jyanvi had been woken up and summoned forthwith to the Matriarch's chambers. She now stared at the Matriarch, Saraswati and the Blue Donkey. 'Did Valerie corrupt the morals of the Ashans?' She repeated the Matriarch's question stupidly. She wasn't sure she had heard right.

'Well?' said the Matriarch. 'Did she? Why is Asha so furious? What happened this morning? What did Valerie say to the Ashans?'

'Nothing much happened,' Jyanvi replied. 'Valerie tried to explain the customs of her own country – I mean where she grew up - but Madhu and Mohan didn't understand, and so she got a bit excited. You know what she's like. That's all.'

Saraswati cleared her throat. 'The charge seems to be that Valerie incited Madhu and Mohan to declare war on Maya.'

Jyanvi was puzzled. 'But she didn't. You heard her. You were there. And in any case I thought we were looking for allies to regain Maya. So even if she had, what would it matter? Is the Apostate really upset?'

'Yes,' responded Asha, sweeping into the Matriarch's chambers, 'your friend has been teaching my poor innocent boys to make war on all women. Apparently that is the practice in the country she comes from.'

Up to this point Jyanvi had thought that there had been some absurd misunderstanding, but now she looked at the Blue Donkey uneasily. The Blue Donkey returned her gaze and said to her in a low voice, 'You see, Valerie has acquainted the young Ashans with the concepts of slavery, rape and war.'

'And the Ashans?' asked Jyanvi.

'Are fascinated.'

Jyanvi didn't know what to say. She was beginning to have some idea of what had happened. She heard the Matriarch speaking to her. 'Go and see Valerie and persuade her to recant.'

Jyanvi was about to protest that Valerie wouldn't understand what she was talking about, but the look in the Matriarch's eye made her realise that that wasn't the point. 'Yes, Aisaheb,' she said meekly, 'I'll go immediately.' Asha the Apostate accompanied her.

They strode down the corridors. As soon as Valerie saw them, she sprang to her feet and demanded to know why she was being treated in this way.

Asha looked at her with distaste. It was obvious that any proximity to Valerie was unpleasant to her. 'You'd better talk to her,' she said to Jyanvi, and left them.

Jyanvi entered the cell and sat down. Valerie had worked herself up into a considerable state. The first step was to calm her down.

'Look,' Jyanvi began, 'it's not a question of justice or injustice, only of perspective. You've got to look at it from their point of view.'

'At what?' Valerie was almost shouting. 'What is it I'm supposed to have done? And why does Asha look at me as though I was some sort of loathsome reptile?'

Suddenly Jyanvi had an idea. She would explain everything to Valerie in terms Valerie would understand.

'You were brought up as a Christian, weren't you?' Jyanvi asked.

'Yes,' Valerie snapped. 'But what's that got to do with anything? I thought you were supposed to be trying to help.'

'I am,' Jyanvi told her. 'Don't you see, from Asha's point of view, you're the serpent in her Garden of Eden. You've made her precious boys eat of the fruit of the tree of knowledge, and now they're corrupted.'

Valerie stared at Jyanvi incredulously. 'Did Asha the Apostate say all that?'

'No, of course not,' Jyanvi replied. 'She's never heard of the Garden of Eden and all the rest. I was just trying to make you understand.'

'Understand what?' Valerie asked in rage and exasperation.

'Look, do calm down and listen for a moment.' Jyanvi patted Valerie's arm. 'You told the Ashans about the norms of a heterosexual patriarchy. Isn't that right?'

'Yes. So what? They seemed revolted,' Valerie said bitterly.

'Well, perhaps they were by some aspects, but they were also fascinated. Don't you see, you gave them knowledge.'

'Knowledge of what?'

'Knowledge of other possibilities,' Jyanvi explained, 'The knowledge that things might be other than they are. You put certain ideas into their heads.'

'What ideas?' asked Valerie. She felt completely baffled. Of what was she being accused?

'The ideas of rape, slavery and war,' Jyanvi replied.

'I did nothing of the sort!' Valerie cried.

'But don't you remember? You described these concepts. And what you didn't describe they worked out for themselves.'

'But I didn't say that any of these ideas were good,' Valerie protested. 'I meant no harm. There was no evil intent.'

'I don't know that the serpent made any specific recommendations,' Jyanvi said drily. 'It wasn't necessary.'

'But I left that society and those norms. I suffered from them!' Valerie was finding it hard to believe that what she had said could be so misconstrued.

'The serpent suffered, too,' Jyanvi pointed out. 'Can't you imagine a conversation in which the serpent is told that what might have proved too much for sensitive serpents would do very well for ordinary men?'

Valerie stared at Jyanvi in horror. 'What are you saying?'

'I'm saying,' Jyanvi told her, 'that you described a society in which there were male masters and female slaves. For you then to say that it was a horrible place makes perfect sense from your point of view, but it doesn't necessarily do so from the point of view of the Ashans.'

'But Mohan and Madhu were both so nice,' Valerie wailed. 'Surely you're not saying that they want to rape and kill...'

'Oh, no, no,' Jyanvi replied. 'Just artificial insemination and enslavement probably.'

Valerie still found it hard to believe. 'Are you saying that the Ashans have actually worked all this out?'

Jyanvi shook her head. 'No, but there's speculation, and a natural concern about their self-interest.'

'What are we to do?' Valerie had lost her sense of outrage. Her voice sounded fearful.

'Find a way of convincing males that a male-dominated society is not in their interests.' Jyanvi felt sorry for Valerie, but in explaining the problem, she had understood it only too well herself.

'But is that possible?' Valerie asked.

'I don't know,' Jyanvi muttered. She added more gently, 'Try to sleep now and get some rest.'

14

It's a privilege

The following morning the helicopter landed. The Mayans and the Ashans had been holding a meeting in the Council Chamber when a dozen soldiers sprang out of the machine, burst into the Chamber and covered everyone with machine guns. 'We come in peace,' announced the leader.

Asha the Apostate recovered first. 'Put down those guns, you fool!' she shouted.

'Put down yours first,' the leader replied.

'We haven't got any guns!' Asha told him. 'Put away those guns before you manage to hurt someone.'

'Okay,' the leader agreed. 'Since you haven't got any guns, we'll put away ours.' The soldiers stopped pointing their machine guns at the Ashans and the Mayans.

'Who are you? Why have you come and how did you get here?' Asha the Apostate asked the leader.

'We're Traders. We've come to trade, and we got here by tuning in on an SOS beam.'

Asha stared at him. There had been something almost mechanical about his speech. 'An SOS beam?' she queried.

'Yeah, you've got a hostage here who's in jeopardy,' the leader informed her. 'One of our jobs is to free citizens.'

There was some murmuring among the Ashans and Mayans. At last Jyanvi suggested to Asha that perhaps they were talking about Valerie and that she be sent for. This was done. Asha turned to the Trader. 'Yes, we do have a prisoner of sorts, but she's hardly a hostage. She has only been confined for her own good. Did she send you a signal?'

'Yeah. Quite a while ago all citizens from the west who went abroad were automatically equipped with automatic beepers. When they're convinced that their lives are in danger, the beepers beep. Then we rescue them.' He stopped talking. It was obvious to him that the sequence of events was crystal clear.

Just then Valerie was brought in. She looked pale and tired. When she saw the soldiers she shrank back, but the leader called out, 'We've come to rescue you.'

'I don't want to be rescued,' Valerie answered.

'Yes, you do. You sent out a signal. We've come to rescue you,' the leader persisted.

The Matriarch took pity on Valerie. 'If she has said she doesn't want to be rescued, do you have to rescue her?'

'Well, no.' The Trader paused. 'But we'd sure like to.'

'Well you can't,' the Matriarch told him firmly. 'Now, what else do you want?'

'We really came to trade and recruit,' he muttered.

'Right,' said Asha the Apostate who had come to a few conclusions of her own. 'Let's start with the recruitment. Who are you recruiting?'

'Well, what about those two boys over there? They look pretty bright.' The leader pointed to Madhu and Mohan.

'But we're Ashans,' Madhu protested. 'Why should we want to be recruited by you?'

'Because,' Asha the Apostate pronounced each word distinctly, 'you could then have the Ashan privileges in a mixed society that Valerie the Outsider was talking about.'

Madhu turned to Valerie. 'Is that true?'

'Well, yes,' she said. 'I suppose it's true.'

But Mohan was looking at the soldiers doubtfully. 'Who are these people?' he asked Valerie. 'Are they Ashans or Mayans?'

'They're Ashans of the type I described to you,' Valerie said reluctantly.

'Well?' The leader was getting impatient. 'Are you joining or aren't you?'

'What are you offering them?' Asha put in.

'We're not offering anything,' he replied. 'It's a privilege. We've got all we want. It's just that these two fellows looked pretty good to me. I was trying to do them a favour.'

'But if we were to join you, what would happen to us?' Mohan demanded.

The Trader grinned encouragingly. 'Why, given a little time, you'd become one of us.'

'You mean we'd be your fellow Ashans in your society?' Mohan persisted.

'Well, I guess so. What does he mean?' the leader asked Valerie.

'He means would they be treated like men in a male-dominated society.' Valerie spelled it out.

'Oh, sure.' He addressed the others, 'There seems to be some misunderstanding though. We're not men.'

'Are you women?' Saraswati burst out. She sounded horrified.

'Who're you calling women? That's an insult!' the soldier roared. 'No, we're male androids built to a specific stereotype.'

'What is he saying?' Madhu asked.

'He's saying that the real Ashans have stayed behind,' Valerie replied. 'You have to call them men,' she added helpfully.

'Then the real men aren't like you?' Mohan asked.

'Hell, no. We're almost perfect.' The leader strutted a little. 'We're the stereotype to which the real men try to approximate. We're the best.'

'Will we be allowed to become full fledged mothers right away?' Mohan enquired.

The Trader stared at him. 'What do you mean?'

'Will we be proper mothers with grade A status just like you and get our babies right away?' Mohan repeated his question.

In response the leader opened his mouth and closed it again. 'You've got to be kidding,' he said at last. 'Now, for the last time, what do you say?'

'No, thank you,' Madhu replied.

'You sure? You're passing up a great chance.' The leader was finding it hard to believe that anyone would refuse such an opportunity.

'Yes, we're quite sure.' Mohan put his arm around Madhu's shoulder.

The leader frowned. 'Say, are you two gay boys?'

'What is "gay"?' Mohan asked.

'You know, "homos".' When Madhu and Mohan still looked puzzled, the leader went on, 'Do you act like girls? I mean what was all that stuff about wanting to be mothers?'

Mohan looked astonished. 'Everybody wants to be a mother,' he said.

'You've got to be crazy,' the leader decided. 'Forget that I asked you. You can't join us. You're not proper men.'

'But we don't want to join you,' Madhu said.

'That doesn't matter,' the leader replied. 'What I'm saying is that even if you wanted to join us, you wouldn't be allowed to. A proper man doesn't want to be a mother.'

'What does he want then?' asked Madhu politely.

'Well, I guess he just wants a mother in the home – where she belongs,' the leader told him. 'You know, just some place to rest after all that fighting and struggling. Mothering's for the birds. It's women's work.'

At this point Asha the Apostate intervened. She had achieved her purpose, and was beginning to find the leader tedious. 'Since recruitment seems to be out of the question, why don't we take the time to refresh ourselves and then discuss the question of trade?'

'We're androids, we don't need refreshments,' the leader growled. 'We'll wait right here in your Council Chamber until you're ready to negotiate. You've got half an hour.'

The Mayans and Ashans trooped out into the brilliant sunshine. Here there were more soldiers. Some were lounging about, some were chewing gum, some were reading comic books and some were standing guard beside the helicopter. Out of curiosity Madhu peered at the cover of one of the comic books. It portrayed a large metal male rampaging about, while two or three diminutive females, who appeared to be made of flesh and blood, clung to him. 'What does it mean?' Madhu asked, but the soldier only set his jaw until his resemblance to the metal monster became even more marked.

Madhu joined the others who were all standing in a loose group. Asha the Apostate was saying, 'Right, then it's agreed that we want to get rid of these androids as quickly as possible. I'll do my best. The rest of you must help me.'

'It may not be easy,' the Matriarch told her. 'You see, Maya Diip has always been treated as forbidden territory. They've been wanting a foothold for a long time. With Valerie's distress signal, they think they've got it. They won't give it up without a fight of some sort.'

'I'm sorry,' said Valerie.

'It wasn't your fault.' The Matriarch spoke kindly.

'No, in a way it was ours,' Madhu put in. 'We're sorry, too.'

Asha the Apostate was secretly pleased, but all she said was, 'That's fine. But what is it that the traders want?'

'I don't know,' replied the Matriarch, 'but I think the whole of Maya Diip is in serious danger. We should send a warning to the mothers of Maya.'

It seemed absurd to Saraswati to be thinking of trying to help Shyamila and Sarla Devi. On the other hand, the situation kept changing so rapidly that it was difficult to keep track of who might be an ally and who mightn't. She felt uncertain about what to say, and so said nothing at all. It was the Blue Donkey who queried the Matriarch. 'But why are you taking them so seriously? It's true that they take themselves seriously, but surely we needn't?'

'Because stupidity is dangerous,' the Matriarch replied. 'They're automated. Any opposition would trigger their machine guns.'

'Couldn't we try to disarm them?' Mohan asked.

'Yes, and seize the helicopter,' Saraswati added.

'I suspect,' the Matriarch told them quietly, 'that the automated response would be almost instantaneous. I think it would be wiser to find out a little more.'

They returned to the Council Chamber. 'Well,' said the leader, 'are you ready to trade?'

'What is it that you wish to trade in?' asked the Apostate.

'What are you selling?' the android countered.

'We aren't selling anything,' Asha replied.

'You've got to sell,' the leader remonstrated. 'How else do you think you're going to get dollars? Shiny dollars.' He held up a coin for Asha's benefit.

'We don't want shiny dollars. What would we do with them?'

'Buy guns.' The response was immediate.

'Guns?'

'Yeah. Guns.' The leader decided Asha was slow. He gesticulated with his hands. 'You know, guns, rockets, Big Bangs.'

'Look,' said the Matriarch, 'we don't want shiny dollars.'

'Everybody wants shiny dollars,' the leader replied. 'But if you're refusing to trade with us, why we'll just refuse to trade with you.'

'That's fine then,' Asha seized her chance quickly. 'We are, in fact, refusing to trade, and so it follows that you're refusing as well. You can go home now. It's all over.'

'Wait a minute,' the leader returned. 'You're holding one of our nationals. We can't leave here till you let her go.'

'She's free to go.' Asha was indifferent.

'I don't want to go,' Valerie protested.

The leader said nothing at all, but he signalled to the soldiers and the machine guns were trained once again on the Ashans and Mayans. For a minute nobody spoke and nobody moved.

Then the leader waved his gun at Asha. 'You're the leader, aren't you? Well, you're deposed for obstructing the causes of democracy and justice. We're appointing a new government that'll be more cooperative and loyal to us.'

'I see,' said Asha. 'Well, now that that's done, we'll carry on.' She started to leave the Council Chamber, but was halted by the leader.

'Stop!' he shouted. 'You're under arrest. And you and you,' he added, pointing to the Matriarch and the other women. 'Take them to the 'copter.' He then informed Madhu, that he, Madhu, was in charge until such time as the androids returned, and that he hoped that the young man appreciated that it wasn't okay to be ruled by women. The leader told Valerie that as a good citizen it was her duty to keep an eye on Madhu. They were taking their prisoners to headquarters, but they'd be back soon. Madhu would have protested, but Asha restrained him. 'I think we can handle them,' she whispered. 'Look after things here.'

The Matriarch and her daughters and Jyanvi and the Blue Donkey were herded into the helicopter. As soon as the doors closed and the rotors began spinning, the androids flung themselves against the walls of the machine and plugged themselves in. Then, to the astonishment of the prisoners, they heard the helicopter croon, 'My pretty ones, my babies, are you tired and hungry?' and they heard the androids reply, 'Oooh, yes, Mother, we're hungry and tired and want to lie down.'

15

The helicopter shuddered

After the androids had recovered from their binge they rose to their feet and stowed themselves away inside the cabin, but the senior android seated himself and stretched his legs. He wanted to chat. 'Well,' he began, 'you must have guessed we're not really taking you to a western base.'

'Yes,' Asha replied briefly.

But the Matriarch and the Blue Donkey had decided that it would be just as well to find out more. 'Tell me,' the Blue Donkey sounded fascinated, and she was, in fact, genuinely interested, 'why did you refuse refreshments on Ashagad, and yet, as soon as we entered the 'copter, you immediately proceeded to feed yourselves? That was what you were doing, wasn't it?'

'Oh sure, but the 'copter's juices are different. I mean what the 'copter gives is mother's milk to us.' He looked a little shy. 'You see, the 'copter's our mother, and we're her babies.'

The Matriarch felt the metal struts under her surreptitiously. It was hard to think of the helicopter as a fellow mother, but she said politely, 'Please present our compliments to your mother. When can we have the opportunity to speak with her?'

'Oh, Mom doesn't talk, at least not much,' the leader replied.

'Why not?' enquired the Matriarch.

'Well, I don't know. I guess she's always been too busy feeding us and foraging for us and carrying us about.'

'What about the others?' asked the Blue Donkey.

'Oh, nobody talks much,' the leader replied. 'Just me.'

'And why is that?'

'I don't know,' answered the android. 'I guess I'm exceptional. I don't mean different. I just mean more of everything the others are. I'm Mom's favourite. I've always had double rations.'

'But if the others don't talk, how did you manage to learn to talk?' Jyanvi put in.

The android seemed to be enjoying talking about himself. 'Why, the same way I learned everything else. Don't you understand?'

They shook their heads.

'Well, I've got that on tape. Hang on a second.' The android paused and then reeled off the following speech: 'The truth is we're an Abandoned Experiment. Once we were abandoned we had only two choices: either to disintegrate or to try in some way to shape ourselves. Our mother, the helicopter, in whose belly we were abandoned, chose the latter course. There was an enormous library of videotapes on board and, of course, we were always able to suck in more. This, so to speak, was our pabulum. With this she fed us and shaped us and turned us into men, but not ordinary men; we are modelled on TV heroes.'

'What is TV?' Saraswati wanted to know.

'Something I banned on Maya Diip around about the time you were born,' the Matriarch replied.

Jyanvi leaned forward. 'I know what you mean about the TV heroes. You remind me of them. But since you're not on television and you're not a man, who are you? I mean, when you're not repeating the television lines, what do you think and say?'

The android looked puzzled. 'I can only say the lines I know. I mean how can I say the lines I don't already know? But if you're asking what we call ourselves, well, I've already told you – we're Traders.'

'Why did you want the two young men?' Asha interjected.

'I told you. We were recruiting. There's a lot of wear and

tear. We need replacements. We thought that if we could turn ourselves into TV heroes, then we could probably turn those boys into real life androids.'

'I see. And what about us?' Saraswati enquired.

'Oh, we're going to sell you,' the android replied. 'You're not one of us. You're females.'

'But why are you going to sell us?' Saraswati persisted.

The android was getting cross. 'Because that's our trade. I've already told you. We had to have an occupation. It's part of our identity.'

'Yes, I see that.' Saraswati was doing her best to remain patient. 'In return for selling us what will you gain?'

'Dollars.'

'What do you do with the dollars?'

'We eat them, of course.'

'What?'

'That's right. And when we need them again, we cough them up.' The android stood up. These females didn't know anything. 'You'll see,' he told them. 'We're nearly there.'

Saraswati ventured one more question. 'But where are you taking us?'

'To Paradise. Look, you're making me tired. I need a little feed. Ahhh. I feel . . . wonderful!' The android had staggered to the nearest outlet and had begun to consume quadruple rations.

The engine coughed and restarted, then coughed and spluttered again. The old machine had over-extended herself; she was going to attempt a forced landing. Jyanvi and the others looked down at the sea and at the shoreline in the near distance. They checked the emergency exits and inflated their life jackets. The other androids were stirring now. When they saw the leader gorging himself, they dived towards the remaining outlets and plugged themselves in. It was heyday and holiday. They seemed to be in ecstasy. The helicopter shuddered and plunged downwards.

PART III

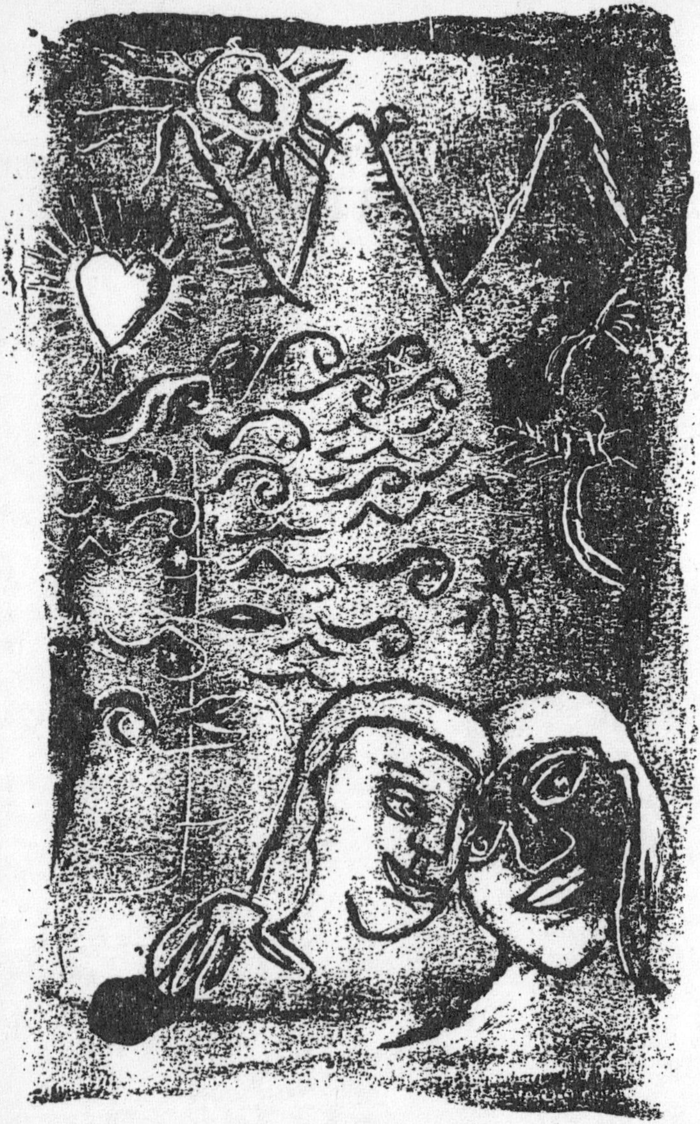

'We've decided that you should be nice to us,'
the Looking Glass creatures informed Alice.
'Why?'
'Because!' they replied triumphantly.

16

Will you have us?

'And is this Paradise?' Saraswati asked.

'Yes,' Jyanvi replied and kissed her.

After the interior of the helicopter, it was pleasant to lie on the sandy beach. It had been easy enough to swim ashore. The 'copter had been close to land and had hovered on the water for a minute or two like a great brooding bird before sinking with her cargo of metal children. Jyanvi and Saraswati were resting in the shade of some coconut trees, while the waves broke against the shore. Presumably this was Paradise, and soon they would have to meet the inhabitants thereof, but for the moment they could relax while their clothes dried in the sun.

The others were sitting some distance away. Asha had one arm around the neck of the Blue Donkey and the other around the Matriarch. It was a great luxury for her to be with her mother again.

After a while Asha said, 'About armies, Mother . . .'

'Yes?'

'Ought we to have one?'

The Matriarch glanced at her eldest curiously. 'What makes you ask?'

'The androids,' Asha replied. 'I told Madhu that we'd be all right, but I had no real plan in my head. The androids were stupid, but they had the guns and we did what they said.' She sounded annoyed with herself.

'That bothered me as well,' the Blue Donkey murmured. 'The problem is, I dislike killing...'

'Killing?' Asha wasn't sure she had heard right.

'Yes, killing,' the Blue Donkey repeated firmly. 'After all, there's no point in having guns, or an army, or wooden rods, or even a strong pair of hind legs, if one isn't willing to use them.'

'But these aren't all the same thing,' Asha protested. 'Besides, what good would your hind legs have been against their guns?'

'I don't know,' the Blue Donkey answered.

Asha turned to the Matriarch. 'Mother?'

'I don't know either,' answered the Matriarch. 'When you were very little and you kicked and screamed, I used to pick you up bodily and set you down in another room... No one got hurt.'

Asha looked at her mother in astonishment. 'Do you want to be as strong as that in relation to everyone and everything else?'

Her mother smiled. 'Like the Blue Donkey, I don't want to kill.'

'But it's one thing to refrain from killing and another thing to be helpless. I mean, could you have killed?' enquired the Blue Donkey. 'Could you have stopped Shyamila, for example? Or the pretty boys? Or the androids?'

'Yes,' said the Matriarch.

Asha and the Blue Donkey stared at her. 'How?' they both asked.

'With a bigger and better gun,' the Matriarch replied. 'It blows up everything for miles around.'

'Including us?' the Blue Donkey said, half incredulous.

The Matriarch smiled, 'Perhaps.'

Asha the Apostate looked at the Matriarch in some perplexity. 'Mother, what are you talking about?'

'The defences of Maya — one of the prerogatives of the Mayan Matriarch,' the Matriarch told her. 'It's all a matter of pressing buttons.'

'What do you mean?'

'There are bombs planted all over the island. There are also means of transporting the bombs. Why do you suppose Maya is forbidden?' The Matriarch sounded weary.

Asha and the Blue Donkey drew away and looked at her in horror. At last Asha asked, 'Why didn't you use them?'

Her mother replied, 'I told you, I find it distasteful.'

For a while nobody said anything.

'Do you suppose,' the Blue Donkey muttered, 'that murder is an acquired skill and has to be taught, or that it comes naturally?'

Suddenly Asha turned on her mother. 'But you killed my pretty boys!' she said wonderingly.

'My dear!' It was hard to read the Matriarch's meaning. Was she merely distressed by the breach of decorum?

They fell silent again. Then the Blue Donkey asked, 'Does Shyamila know?'

'No, she doesn't know.'

'Then hadn't we better get back before she finds out?'

'Perhaps,' replied the Matriarch. 'But it's unlikely that she will; the computers respond to my codes and my combinations. In the Matriarchy of Maya that's the power behind the throne.'

The Blue Donkey looked at the Matriarch. 'Why didn't you use it?'

The Matriarch merely looked back at the Blue Donkey, until at last the Blue Donkey dropped her eyes. Then the Matriarch smiled. 'Tell me,' she said briskly, 'Who do you think I should appoint as my Successor, the woman who would willingly use the power or the one who would not?'

Asha and the Blue Donkey looked away uneasily.

The Matriarch relented. 'Come. Let's discuss something else – the art of poetry, or the blueness of the sea or the nature of the inhabitants of Paradise. Look, here come two of them.'

The others looked in the direction indicated and saw two figures running towards them. When the two runners reached the little group, one of them cried, 'I'm Madhu and she's Mala. Welcome to Paradise. Are you Mothers and can we have you?'

The Matriarch was taken aback, but she answered civilly. 'This is the Blue Donkey, and yes, we're Mothers from Maya. Are you the inhabitants of Paradise?'

'Yes, we are,' replied Madhu. 'I thought you might be Mothers. Can we have you or are you spoken for?'

'What do you mean?'

But just then Jyanvi and Saraswati strolled up. 'Are they Mothers, too?' Mala asked.

'Saraswati is,' the Matriarch replied.

'And the other?'

'The other is her lover,' the Blue Donkey told them.

'Oh, too bad. She's not available. But will you have us?' Madhu asked.

Madhu was kneeling at the Matriarch's feet and Mala was kneeling at Asha's. 'Have you as what?' Asha gazed at them in perplexity.

'As your Gallants, your suitors and supplicants – as your children as it were,' Mala explained.

'But you're grown ups!'

Mala smiled at Asha sweetly. 'Of course,' she said. 'In Paradise there are no real children.'

'But how do you propagate?' Jyanvi cut in.

'Immigration. Lots of people apply to come to Paradise. We only take the fully grown. After all, everything is plentiful in Paradise, except, of course, Mothers. Are you sure you're not a Mother?' Mala smiled at Jyanvi hopefully.

'No, I'm not,' Jyanvi replied brusquely. 'But if you're all grown ups, why do you want Mothers?'

'Don't you want a Mother?' Mala looked at her hopefully.

'No!'

'Then can we have her?'

'Who?'

Mala pointed to Saraswati.

'No!'

The Blue Donkey intervened. 'Your customs are strange to us,' she said peaceably. 'Are we to understand that you're making a request of the Matriarch and Asha?'

'Oh, yes,' Madhu replied. 'We saw the 'copter crash and ran to the beach in order to be first.'

'And would it be in order for the Matriarch and for Asha to refuse your request?' continued the Blue Donkey.

'The longer they refuse, the longer we can woo them,' Madhu told her gleefully. 'That's the best part.'

'Very well,' said the Blue Donkey. 'They both refuse you at present. Now would you please lead us to some food and shelter and give us a chance to recover ourselves?'

'Of course,' cried Madhu. 'Our pleasure is to serve them – and their friends.'

'It's our duty to suffer in the cause of love,' Mala added.

The Blue Donkey stared at them. 'Are you suffering?'

They nodded vigorously. 'Oh yes!'

'They're mad!' snorted the Blue Donkey.

'They're not mad,' Jyanvi corrected. 'Just romantic.'

'At any rate they're certainly childish. Do you know, five of them sang all night long outside my window,' Saraswati told them. 'They said they were serenading.'

'But I thought that since you have Jyanvi, you were out of the running . . .' The Blue Donkey's voice trailed away.

'Oh no.' Jyanvi explained. 'The fact that she's seemingly inaccessible only makes her more attractive. They're like mosquitoes. But I've made sure that they won't bother me.'

'What did you do?' asked the Blue Donkey.

Jyanvi grinned. 'Well, when one or two of them approached me, I told them that I wasn't in the least bit interested in mothering them, but that if they were interested in mothering me . . .'

'What happened?'

'They fled.'

Saraswati shook her head at Jyanvi. 'That was unkind. They mean no harm. They only want a little attention after all, in return for which –'

'Yes?' Jyanvi asked. 'What do they offer?'

'Their need.'

There was an awkward pause.

Then Jyanvi said, 'In this society there are two categories – Mothers and Gallants. I don't in the least wish to be a Mother; but as for the Gallants – I despise them!'

Jyanvi had spoken with such vehemence that the Blue Donkey gave her a sharp look, but contented herself with saying, 'Come on. Let's go and see if the Matriarch and Asha are awake yet.'

They had each of them been given separate cabins within the compound of a large garden near the beach. The entrance to the Matriarch's cabin was partly blocked by a mountain of paper. There was a similar mountain outside Asha's cabin. Madhu and Mala were helping the two Mayans pick up the paper.

'What is it?' the Blue Donkey asked.

The Matriarch smiled at her, 'It appears to be poetry.'

'Are the inhabitants of Paradise lovers of poetry?' Jyanvi enquired.

'Oh yes,' replied Madhu. 'We write it all the time.'

When they had finished picking up the poetry and had stacked it away, Mala said, 'There are dozens of Gallants outside the garden gates awaiting your pleasure. They want to know what would please you and would be glad to gratify any whim. They've waited all night for just a glimpse of you. Perhaps you'd be kind and grant each one an interview?'

The Blue Donkey came to the Matriarch's rescue. 'Let's discuss the matter,' she said firmly, 'over breakfast.'

The sun shone down on them. The Ranisaheb, Asha the Apostate and Saraswati had each been set up in a striped deck chair under separate palm trees. Long queues trailed away from them towards the ocean. For breakfast Madhu and Mala had offered the castaways a bit of coconut and an orange or two. They seemed to think this was sufficient. Then they had begged them to see their suitors. The Matriarch and her daughters were doing so, while Jyanvi and the Blue Donkey looked on.

After a while Jyanvi and the Blue Donkey approached Mala. 'Please,' the Blue Donkey said, 'our friends are exhausted. This must stop.'

'But we don't mean any harm,' Mala protested. 'Look at the queues. They come from miles around just to be with the Mothers for a short moment. You see, there's a great shortage of Mothers in Paradise.' She looked at Jyanvi doubtfully. 'You don't think you could be one just to help out?'

'No!' replied Jyanvi violently. 'But tell me, why is there a shortage of Mothers? Is there some reluctance to take on that role? And if so, why?'

'Yes.' Mala scowled. 'Yes, there is reluctance, and I don't know why and what's more I don't want to talk about it. As for the queues, I'll see what I can do. I'll try to arrange for an interval.'

Just then they heard a low purring, quite distinct from the crashing of the waves. Twelve Rolls Royces were gliding across the sands towards the Matriarch. The chauffeurs got out and stood at attention. Their leader knelt and declared solemnly, 'The Queen of Paradise sends greetings to the Matriarch of Maya and begs that the Distinguished Visitor and her Entourage will honour her by being her guests.'

'Yes, thank you,' responded the Matriarch and let the poem with which the hundredth suitor had just presented her slide off her lap.

'We will escort you,' went on the Queen's Representative. 'For your transport the Queen has sent a fleet of Rolls. Will they be suitable?'

'Yes, thank you,' replied the Matriarch again, and in no time at all the others were summoned and they prepared to set off. For some reason, instead of being disappointed, the suitors regarded this as an occasion for celebration. They cheered and whistled and garlanded the cars; then, amid much singing and dancing and merry making, they accompanied the procession on its way to the palace.

17

The poetic thing

The Queen of Paradise turned out to be a sensible person. The Blue Donkey sighed with relief, as did Jyanvi and the others. She greeted them cheerfully, saw to it that they were comfortably settled and gave them a chance to rest before dinner. 'I would have been happier to see you under better circumstances,' she told them. 'The truth is, there's a crisis in Paradise and I am in desperate need of help, but more of that later.'

Their chambers were oddly furnished, their bath water was tepid and the dinner itself was barely edible. None of this surprised them greatly. They had learnt already that in Paradise very little worked. The procession had broken down several times and two of the cars had had to be pushed. At least they were rid of the suitors for the time being, and for this they were indebted to the Queen. She had seen to it that the palace doors were firmly shut. They felt sorry for her. After dinner she confided in them.

'You will have guessed at the problems of Paradise,' she began.

Jyanvi thought that she would now speak of the shortage of mothers. The Blue Donkey thought that she would say something about the inefficiency of the system, and the others thought that she would express her concern over the childishness of the

Gallants. What she actually said startled them all: 'The Children of Paradise are killing themselves.'

'Do you mean that literally?' the Matriarch enquired.

'Yes. Let me give you an example. Do you remember the two young people you first encountered on the beach?'

'Yes, of course. Madhu and Mala.'

'Well, Mala is dead. She threw herself off one of the turrets soon after you arrived here.'

The Matriarch was horrified. 'The poor child!' she cried out. 'Why did she do such a thing?'

The Queen shrugged. 'For me these things have become everyday occurrences and have lost their horror. She left the usual Suicide Poem behind.'

'What is a Suicide Poem?' Jyanvi asked.

'When the Gallants commit suicide, they leave behind a couplet, sometimes a quatrain.' The Queen shrugged once again. 'It has become a custom, a tradition – the poetic thing to do – to die with a song on your lips.'

'And what did Mala's note say?' asked the Matriarch.

'Forgive me if I tell you that I cannot remember exactly. It was like hundreds of others. Something like:

> "Now that I have seen her at last,
> My life is done, my pleasures past." '

'But what does it mean?' asked the Blue Donkey.

'I think it's supposed to be a tribute to beauty,' Jyanvi whispered to her.

'Whose beauty?' the Blue Donkey whispered back.

'Ideal beauty – as well as yours, of course.' The Queen nodded in the direction of Asha. 'According to our legends Paradise was founded by a Princess of Maya who sailed away in search of happiness. Do you know the tale? An extreme idealism is fundamental to Paradise.'

'But if the Children of Paradise are willing to die for their ideals, what is the problem?' The Blue Donkey was genuinely puzzled.

The Queen of Paradise turned to her. 'The problem is they won't live for them. Perhaps you will understand Paradise better if I tell you the tale of the Princess Jaya and her Shobha Rani.'

Both Asha and Saraswati let out an exclamation. It was Saraswati who spoke. 'But the story of the Runaway Princess and her Beauty Queen is a well-known cautionary tale. She was the one who was debarred from the throne for being such a fool, wasn't she?'

The Queen of Paradise smiled and threw a reassuring glance at the Matriarch as though to say, 'It's all right, the child hasn't offended me.' She explained to Saraswati, 'According to the legends of Paradise, the Princess Jaya nobly spurned the throne of Maya Diip for the sake of Beauty.'

'Was Beauty another Mayan Princess?' asked the Blue Donkey, who was trying to keep the story clear in her head.

'No, Beauty was a statue!' Saraswati replied scornfully.

'That's right,' the Queen of Paradise agreed. 'The Victorious Princess and the Beauty Queen sailed away with no money at all and a fair wind, and landed in Paradise.'

'But what did she do with the statue?' the Blue Donkey whispered.

'Worshipped it,' Jyanvi whispered back.

'Yes, that's right,' the Queen of Paradise said. 'She worshipped it.'

'And then what happened?' asked the Blue Donkey.

'Then the Beauty Queen came to life.'

'And then?'

'And then the Victorious Princess took her in her arms.'

'And then?'

'And then they both died.' The Queen of Paradise finished the tale.

'Why?' demanded the Blue Donkey indignantly.

'That was the penalty,' replied the Queen. 'It's part of the story. You see, you have to understand that for the Children of Paradise death is definitive.'

'Oh.' The Blue Donkey thought it over. 'What about the Mothers?' she asked.

'The Mothers according to legend must be worshipped,' the Queen told her. 'As you see, our society is neatly divided into Mothers and Gallants.'

'But the Mothers aren't real mothers, of course,' Asha the Apostate interjected.

The Queen of Paradise raised her eyebrows. 'What do you mean?'

'We were told,' Asha said carefully, 'that there are no real children in Paradise.'

'No, of course there aren't,' the Queen replied. 'That would spoil everything.'

'But surely being a Mother *vis-à-vis* a Gallant must be a very different thing from looking after a real child?' Asha insisted.

'What's your experience?' the Queen of Paradise countered. 'A Gallant, after all, is a grown-up person, whose first duty is service.'

'But there seems to be a problem?' Asha suggested.

'Yes, there is.' The Queen's voice had acquired a certain sharpness. 'In the absence of real children, the Gallants have become increasingly childish. In my experience mothering childish grown-ups is at least as arduous as any other mothering.'

'Are the rewards as great?' asked Jyanvi suddenly.

'Obviously not,' replied the Queen. 'As you can see, there's a surplus of Gallants and a shortage of Mothers in Paradise.'

The Matriarch had been listening to this interchange thoughtfully. 'Are immigrants to Paradise given a choice?' she enquired.

'Oh yes,' answered the Queen. 'The Pursuit of Beauty, Love, Freedom and Happiness – these are the inalienable rights of the citizens of Paradise. So naturally they have a choice. When they first enter Paradise, they choose their role for the next ten years. After that they must change roles, and it's usually at that point that they commit suicide.'

'But is the suicide rate of the young ones the problem, or is the problem the shortage of mothers?' asked the Blue Donkey, trying to get it straight.

'Both,' said the Queen of Paradise. 'I think they're connected.

The Gallants despair of winning a Mother for themselves before they have to take on the job of mothering.'

'But can't the Gallants pair with one another? Then if we could somehow prevent them from killing themselves — or each other — we'll have solved the problem.' The Blue Donkey sounded hopeful.

'In Paradise,' the Queen explained, 'the roles are clearly differentiated and two of a kind may not pair. That would be wrong. I know that the customs of Maya are entirely different. On your island there are only Mothers and no Gallants, so things are otherwise . . . I must say I was a little surprised when I was told that a member of your party professed to be a Gallant.' She threw a glance at Jyanvi.

Jyanvi frowned. 'I didn't say I was a Gallant,' she mumbled. 'I just said I didn't want to be a Mother.'

The Matriarch intervened. 'If the numbers of Gallants and Mothers were more or less equal, would the number of suicides drop, do you think?'

'I think so,' replied the Queen of Paradise. 'You see, according to the Suicide Poems most of them say they are killing themselves out of unrequited love.'

'But is that true?' Jyanvi put it.

'Well, it may be,' Saraswati responded. 'After all, it's only another way of saying that they haven't been coddled and mothered enough.' Jyanvi looked at her sharply, and then looked away.

'I'm a little confused about the gender of the Gallants.' Asha the Apostate broached the subject hesitantly. 'Are they male or female? I mean would my Ashans be welcome here?'

The Queen of Paradise seemed surprised. 'Of course they'd be welcome, particularly if they were willing to start out as Mothers. Since Paradise was founded by a Mayan Princess we use the feminine gender for everyone. In Paradise that's not a matter of any consequence. In Paradise it's whether you're a Gallant or a Mother that makes the real difference. Would your Ashans like to come here as Mothers by any chance?'

'The problem is,' Asha said awkwardly, 'my Ashans want real children.'

The Queen of Paradise shook her head. 'No, that won't do at all.'

The Blue Donkey spoke suddenly, 'Even as we sit here talking, are thousands of Gallants killing themselves?'

'Yes.'

'Couldn't you order them to stop? As Queen of Paradise many of them must owe you allegiance.'

'I've done that already,' the Queen told her.

'And the effect?'

'It has reduced the numbers.' The Queen shrugged. 'Some kill themselves anyway and make a point of the paradox. Others just sulk. Meanwhile, the systems of Paradise are in dissolution and Paradise must soon fall apart.'

'What do you mean?' asked Saraswati.

'Well, you see, the Gallants of Paradise only work when inspired,' the Queen explained, 'and the few remaining Mothers are on the point of collapse.'

'Why don't you order the Gallants to work?' Saraswati suggested. 'Isn't "service" their motto? And aren't they supposed to be gratified when they find an opportunity of serving you?'

The Queen looked at them helplessly. 'I've tried that as well, but it means having to issue an order for every single bit of work; and then having to spend time afterwards acknowledging the service and doling out favours. It's tedious – and inefficient. The Princess Jaya called this Paradise because the soil was so fertile, the climate so balmy; but to live here does require a little work.'

'There's only one solution.' The Matriarch looked directly at the Queen.

The Queen hesitated. 'We have thought of it,' she said at last, 'but it would mean that Paradise would cease to be paradisial.' She sighed. 'People would no longer be able to devote themselves exclusively to the Pursuit of Beauty and Freedom and Love and Happiness.'

'At least they'd survive,' the Matriarch retorted.

'What are they talking about?' Jyanvi whispered.

'I think they're talking about bringing in real children,' the Blue Donkey whispered back.

'But that would make for a different set of problems!' Jyanvi exclaimed.

'Yes,' the Blue Donkey murmured, 'that's what the Queen of Paradise is saying.'

When they eventually retired for the night, Saraswati said that she had a headache and would prefer to sleep alone. Jyanvi merely nodded. She wasn't going to be forced into being a Mother, but she'd be damned if she'd beg like any Gallant in Paradise.

18

What's your part?

Jyanvi woke up to the sound of bugles. The Blue Donkey was shaking her. 'Wake up! The Queen of Paradise and the Matriarch are up to something. They're out there on the ramparts addressing a crowd of cheering Gallants. Hurry! I want to hear what they're saying.'

Jyanvi tumbled out of bed and rushed after the Blue Donkey. Saraswati and Asha were already in the corridor wanting to know what was happening. 'It's the Matriarch and the Queen,' the Blue Donkey told them as she dashed past.

They got there just in time to hear the Matriarch shouting, 'Are you brave and trusty Gallants?'

An enthusiastic cheer rose up from below. 'Yaaay!'

'Do you adore the Queen of Paradise?'

'Yaaay!'

The Queen of Paradise stepped forward and addressed them next. 'Do you adore the Mother of the Mayan Isle?'

'Yaaay!'

'But she's in danger.'

'Nooo.'

'Yes, she is. Will you defend her with your lives?'

'Yaaay!'

'Are you brave and trusty Gallants?'

'Yaaay!'

'Are you willing to fight?'

'Yaaay!'

'Then you must go with her and help her to regain her lost birthright.'

The cheers had been growing progressively louder, and this last suggestion was received with the greatest enthusiasm.

Below them the Gallants cheered and roared and stamped their feet. Jyanvi and the Blue Donkey looked at one another. 'But why are they so pleased?' Jyanvi asked.

'I think,' replied the Blue Donkey, 'it's because they've finally found a glorious way of killing themselves.'

All that morning Jyanvi and the Blue Donkey roamed the corridors in the hope of having a word with the Matriarch, or, failing that, at least with the Queen of Paradise. But the palace was in an uproar and the two queens were busy. Each was constantly surrounded by a group of Gallants, who would listen attentively and then scurry away, intent on business. As these groups dispersed they were immediately replaced by other Gallants. Towards mid-day the Blue Donkey noticed that the Gallants were beginning to form their own groups. Despairing of ever getting close to the Matriarch, Jyanvi and the Blue Donkey approached one of these groups.

Madhu was at the centre and she was earnestly addressing a dozen Gallants. 'We are the Avians. I'm your Chief, and you're my captains. Do you understand?' She glared into their faces. 'Our colours are scarlet and black. We are the Avians, the élite of the corps. We shall descend on Maya Diip like the silver rain. None can resist us. The Mayan Queen shall reign again. We are her warriors.'

'I say,' said the Blue Donkey when the cheering had died. 'What are you going on about? Who are you fighting and what are you fighting for?'

'Don't you know?' Madhu looked surprised. Then she assumed an exalted expression. 'We're fighting for Justice and Peace. We're fighting to restore the Mayan Queen to the Mayan throne.'

The Blue Donkey looked at her curiously. 'Exactly how do you propose to do all that?' she asked.

'With fire, air and water,' Madhu replied grandly. 'We're the Warriors of Air. We shall fight with the most dazzling display of light and colour.'

'War isn't a game, you know,' Jyanvi put it mildly.

'Life is a game,' responded Madhu gaily. 'We are Gallants.' With that she tossed a plumed hat high into the air and her captains followed suit.

The Blue Donkey hesitated. She wanted to warn the young woman, to make her come to her senses. 'Look, Madhu,' she said gently, 'have you thought about what you're doing? Can't you see that you're only striking an attitude and that it's dangerous?'

That tore it. Madhu drew herself up and looked down on the Blue Donkey and on Jyanvi with immense disdain. 'It's you we're protecting,' she said coldly. 'You ought to be grateful.' She turned her back on them while the Avian captains shouldered them out.

'We must do something,' the Blue Donkey muttered.

Jyanvi looked uncertain. 'But if this is the Matriarch's doing – ' she began.

'Of course it's the Matriarch's doing,' the Blue Donkey interrupted. 'The Queen of Paradise and the Ranisaheb have thought of this scheme between them. Don't you see? It gives the Gallants a sense of purpose. They're actually working. They have something to do. Look. That group there is talking about transport. That one in the corner is talking about communications. They've been given a cause.'

'But that's good, isn't it?' Jyanvi responded. 'Presumably the suicide rate will drop. And if some of these Gallants march away to Maya Diip, that will reduce the population imbalance.'

'Of course, there are some good effects,' the Blue Donkey muttered. 'That's why they thought of it.'

'Well, then what's your objection?' Jyanvi asked.

The Blue Donkey frowned. 'It's obvious, isn't it? I'm thinking of the wasted lives of the young Gallants.'

'They won't necessarily get killed, you know,' Jyanvi pointed out.

'Yes, that's true. I'm certain that the Matriarch will do everything she can to avoid an actual confrontation,' the Blue Donkey replied thoughtfully. 'I doubt very much that she wants the Gallants on Mayan soil...'

'And the Queen of Paradise doesn't want them here,' Jyanvi murmured. 'But I wonder what the two intend to do with them once they've served their purpose?'

This had the effect of making the Blue Donkey look sadder than ever. 'Let's see if we can find Saraswati and Asha the Apostate,' she muttered. 'Perhaps they'll have a better idea of what's going on.'

They found Saraswati and Asha enthroned on a platform in one of the great halls. Gallants were rushing to and fro. The procedure seemed to be that a Gallant would approach, kneel before the two women, speak briefly and add to the pile of documents that lay before them.

Jyanvi and the Blue Donkey pushed their way through the throng. When they got to the platform, a guard halted them.

'Kneel before the Mothers of Maya,' the guard commanded.

'Nonsense,' replied the Blue Donkey. The guard began to beat her down.

Luckily, Asha the Apostate noticed the commotion. 'It's all right,' she called out. 'Let them approach.'

'What's going on?' demanded the Blue Donkey when at last they had reached Saraswati and Asha.

Jyanvi eyed the pile of documents. 'Are they giving you more poems?'

Saraswati answered her, 'No, those are lists.' She sounded tired.

'Lists?'

'Yes, lists. They may contain a poem or two, but they're mostly lists,' Saraswati told her.

'Lists of what?' Jyanvi asked.

'Lists of the materials and preparations needed for the war.'

'The war?'

'Don't parrot everything I say,' Saraswati snapped. 'Surely you've realised that the Gallants have decided to come to our rescue and to march on Maya? I'm sorry,' she added. 'I didn't mean to snap. It's just that all this – ' she indicated the scene around her – 'is a bit much.'

'But what's your part in it?' the Blue Donkey wanted to know.

Asha looked at her steadily. 'We've been set up.'

'Can't you stop it?' the Blue Donkey protested.

'No, I don't think so,' Asha replied. 'Not once the machinery has been set in motion. Besides, do we want to stop it?'

'But what are you going to do?' The Blue Donkey's voice was troubled.

'I'm going to join in and try to control it in order to ensure minimal damage.' Asha the Apostate answered grimly. 'You'd better do the same.'

'I don't like killing.' The Blue Donkey said obstinately.

'In that case it's as well you're in charge of the food supplies and the medical wing. You've been appointed Supplier General and Chief of the Medical Corps.'

'I see.' The Blue Donkey took in the news. 'What if I refuse?'

'What would be the point?' Asha indicated a pile of documents and a group of Gallants. 'They're your concern. At least you'll be able to help them. Better get to work.'

The Blue Donkey hesitated, but then she slowly cleared a space for herself and summoned the Gallants. She got down to work.

Jyanvi watched in silence. 'What about me?' she asked at last. 'Haven't I got a job?'

'Of course you have,' Asha replied. 'You are the Commander-in-Chief of the Allied Forces of Air, Fire and Water.'

'Me? Why me?' Jyanvi was taken by surprise.

'Well, that's what the Matriarch and the Queen decided. Perhaps it's because out of all of us, you're most like the Gallants.' Saraswati said this without any sarcasm, but it hurt Jyanvi.

'I'm not a swashbuckler!' she responded angrily.

'That's just as well,' Asha soothed her. 'Perhaps you'll be able to keep them from harm.'

'But what's my job?' Jyanvi demanded.

'Your first duty is to look magnificent,' Asha informed her. 'A suitable costume has been designed for you. As soon as you're able, put it on.' Jyanvi grimaced and was about to protest, but Asha continued relentlessly. 'Your next duty is to make sure that the Gallants think highly of themselves. So they, too, must be dressed splendidly. Check their uniforms and inspect them daily. Make sure they parade themselves.'

Jyanvi glanced at the Gallants in the hall. 'They already think well of themselves.'

'Yes,' Asha agreed. 'Your job should be easy.'

'Is that all I have to do?' Jyanvi asked.

'No,' Asha told her. 'You have to work out a strategy.'

'A strategy?'

'That's right, a strategy,' Asha repeated. 'For reinstating the Matriarch. And when that's done, for disposing of the Gallants.'

'I see,' said Jyanvi thoughtfully. 'Well, perhaps I'd better begin. Where are the Chiefs of Air, Fire and Water?' She didn't feel entirely happy about her job, but at least she had one. It occurred to her that Madhu would have to be more respectful in future.

'I think,' Asha suggested gently, 'that you'd better put on your costume first.'

'Why?'

'Because without it, it's highly unlikely that they'll obey your commands,' Asha pointed out. She smiled to take the sting out of her remark.

'All right,' Jyanvi agreed.

She went off to change. The Blue Donkey drudged on. And Asha and Saraswati sat there patiently receiving adulation.

For the next fortnight everyone was busy. There was no time for conversation. It seemed to Jyanvi that the others, especially the Matriarch and the Blue Donkey, were avoiding her. When she mentioned this to the Blue Donkey, the Blue Donkey said that the Matriarch was avoiding everyone. But surely tonight, Jyanvi thought, after the Grand Parade, the Matriarch would agree to a council of war, at least to some sort of discussion. After all, they were setting off tomorrow. Meanwhile, Jyanvi sweltered in her grand uniform and tried to look equally grand as she watched the display of the Allied Forces.

The Avians, the Fire Throwers and the Water Workers had competed eagerly. The weapons they had thought of were many and ingenious. Some were secret, like the Great Magnifying Glass. The idea was that the Avians were to extend it over Maya Nagar and thus reduce the city to cinders. Then there was the plan that the Water Workers had conceived of producing a tidal wave that would inundate the whole island. These were, of course, as the designers had insisted, ultimate weapons, only to be used as a last resort, only as threats . . . There were, they admitted, still flaws in the designs – the tidal wave was not properly directional, the magnifying glass needed to be made of some lightweight material – but they were working on them.

Jyanvi squirmed under her cloak. More and more she had come to hate trying to behave like an Arch-Gallant. What was she to do? When the time came, how was she going to control the Forces? The Fire Throwers and the Water Workers were putting on a show, which, in spite of herself, she found beautiful. Jets of fire and jets of water arched and intersected and swung around with military precision. She glanced at Saraswati, but Saraswati was absorbed in the spectacle. Of late Saraswati had had less and less to say to her. Only Asha and the Blue Donkey had been kind, but they too had been busy. Jyanvi suppressed a sigh. She straightened her shoulders, held up her chin and tried to look fierce and confident.

She glanced around her. In the royal box the Queen of Paradise was smiling down upon the Gallants. In the distance scarlet blimps with black markings stood out against a blue sky. She knew that each blimp was tethered to a motorboat rocking in the harbour. This was to be their means of transport. Tomorrow they would set off for Maya Diip. But surely before that the Matriarch must speak to her, must give her some private instructions? Not over dinner. Dinner would be a formal occasion, and the Allied Chiefs would all be present. But surely after dinner?

Dinner came and went and nothing happened. Jyanvi went to bed in an uneasy frame of mind. When at last she fell asleep, she had an unpleasant dream. The mothers of Maya had pricked the blimps with little needles. This had released a rain of blood, which covered the island like paint. The blood stank and was sticky. The nausea woke her. It was already five in the morning. She might as well get up. She sat down on the floor in the lotus position and breathed deeply in an effort to calm down. Then she put on the uniform which defined her position.

19

Write a poem

In spite of herself Jyanvi felt her spirits rising. The shehnai sounded triumphant and sensual. The drums thundered. The Mothers of Paradise cheered the Gallants, as did the Gallants who stayed behind (for necessary war work). The Queen of Paradise shed her blessings on everyone. The Gallants themselves looked happy and gay in their pretty uniforms, their gorgeous colours. For a moment Jyanvi felt a surge of pride that she was to be the leader of this grand expedition. Then her heart sank again. And then she decided to suspend thought for the next little while. The blimps were lowered, the Gallants mounted, flags fluttered and by noon the process of loading was done. The green motorboats with the scarlet stripe were within the provenance of the Water Workers. They were in readiness, and in no time at all the first of these set off with the flagship in tow. The rest followed in formation.

In addition to the regular crew, the flagship carried the Matriarch of Maya, Asha the Apostate, the Princess Saraswati, the Blue Donkey and Her Excellency, Jyanvi, the Commander-in-Chief of the Allied Forces. It was about the size of a blue whale. Above them the clouds scudded by, below them the sea was a peaceful and sequinned blue. It would take them two hours to reach Maya Diip. Perhaps the Matriarch would talk to her now, Jyanvi wondered. There was no one else in the cabin at the moment. Jyanvi glanced in the Matriarch's direction without much hope and the Matriarch actually smiled at her. Jyanvi smiled back tentatively. The Matriarch patted the seat beside her. 'Come and sit down,' she said. 'You look anxious.'

Jyanvi sat down.

'Now,' said the Matriarch pleasantly, 'what's the matter?'

Jyanvi thought for a second. 'Well, it's our strategy that's worrying me . . .' Her voice trailed away.

'Yes?' The Matriarch's voice was encouraging.

Jyanvi pulled herself together. 'The Giant Magnifying Glass and the Directional Tidal Wave haven't been perfected yet, though they're working on them. I suppose we could bluff and use them as a threat?' Her voice became anxious. 'Or there are the atomic devices you control. Those would be a genuine threat. We're going to use threats, aren't we?' She looked at the Matriarch doubtfully.

The Matriarch smiled. 'No,' she replied, 'we're not going to use threats, atomic or otherwise.'

'But what are we going to do?' By now Jyanvi was in a state of considerable distress. 'I don't want to kill the Mayan mothers or the Gallants of Paradise!' she cried. 'Don't you see? There's going to be the most horrifying bloodshed.'

Jyanvi sobbed and for a minute or two the Matriarch comforted her against her breast. 'It's all right,' she consoled. 'It's all right. You're relieved of your command, or rather superseded. I'll take over. Now, there are only two tasks you have to perform.'

'What?' Jyanvi asked through her tears.

'The first is to make sure that the communications system is in working order,' the Matriarch told her.

'It is,' Jyanvi replied. 'But I'll make sure.'

'And the second is to write a poem.'

'What?' Jyanvi exclaimed, incredulous. Was the Matriarch making fun of her?

'Write a poem,' the Matriarch repeated.

'At a time like this?'

'Yes.' The Matriarch appeared to be serious. 'It's necessary.'

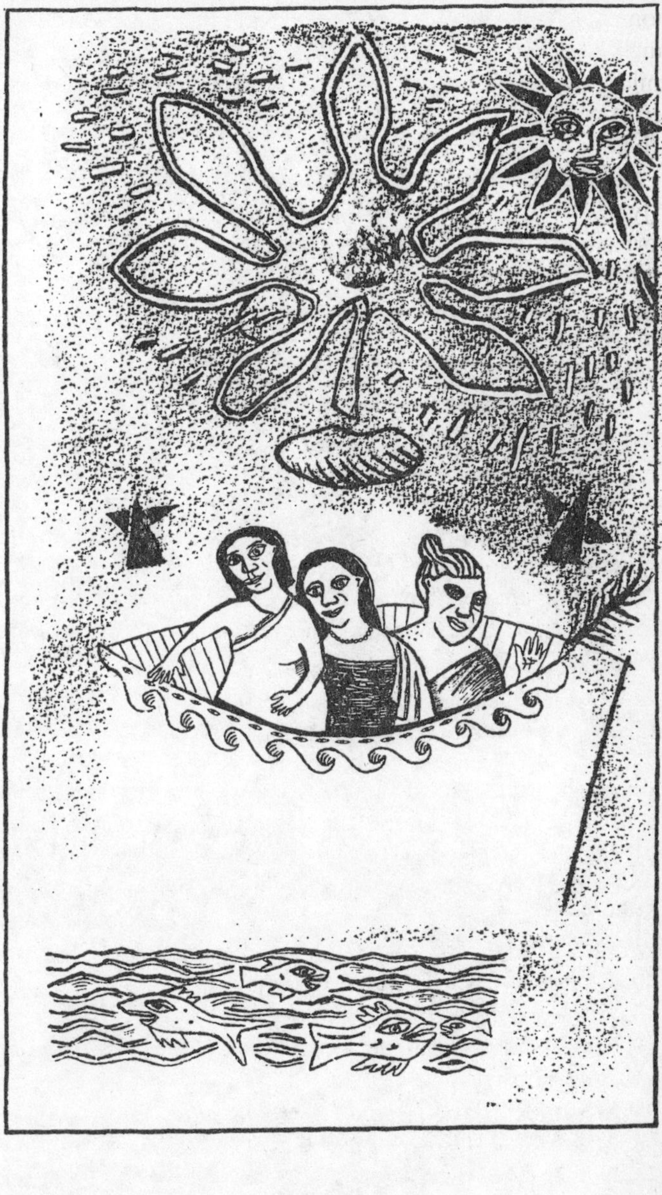

'What sort of poem?' Jyanvi asked feebly.

'It will have to be an epic, I think,' the Matriarch said casually. 'And it must describe the valour and splendour of the Gallants.'

'An epic!' Jyanvi stared. Had the Matriarch suddenly become irresponsible? 'How long do I have to complete it?'

'Nearly an hour,' replied the Matriarch. 'It must be ready before we arrive above Maya Diip.'

'It can't be done.' Jyanvi was definite.

'Yes, it can.' The Matriarch instructed her. 'Begin with a description of each of the blimps, then of their pilot boats, then of the heroic attributes of the chiefs, the captains and the other officers. Embroider and embellish and carry on in this way. The remaining sections can be left blank. They're to be the chapters of a Voyage of Discovery. Surely you have an outfit of Slogan Writers? Give them the outline and tell them to fill it in later.'

Jyanvi gaped at the Matriarch. 'But you've already given me the outline.'

'Yes. That should make your task easier. Now, go on.' She patted Jyanvi's shoulder. 'Get to work.'

Jyanvi went away and settled down with a piece of paper. 'Of the ships that sailed from Paradise,' she began, 'these were the emblems that distinguished each one . . .'

As they approached Maya Diip, the Matriarch took her place at the helm. Her daughters flanked her, and Jyanvi and the Blue Donkey stood just behind.

'Are the amplifiers ready? Good. Switch on the communications.' The Matriarch's orders were promptly relayed and carried out. 'Now navigate us so that we remain stationary just above the Great Cave Temple. Tell the rest of the fleet to remain offshore in an arrow formation which points to us.'

Jyanvi wondered what the red arrow must look like to the Mayans on the ground. The Matriarch had begun to speak. Her voice must be rolling through the Mayan streets. The amplifiers had been set for maximum volume.

'O Mothers of Maya,' the Matriarch's voice thundered down, 'your Matriarch has been on a state visit to the Queen of

Paradise. Now she returns. She brings with her two Mayan daughters, the Princess Saraswati and the Princess Asha. They are escorted by the Gallants of Paradise. Bid them welcome.'

A great cheer rose up from the ground. The Mayans had been told that the Matriarch had gone to the forest. That she had been to Paradise instead and was now back with a friendly armada was even better. They were glad to have her back. The rule of Shyamila the Civil and Sarla Devi had not been popular.

The Matriarch spoke again. 'I am glad to be back.' Below her the Mayans cheered.

'Let my daughters Pramila and Shyamila ascend the platform so that they may be reunited with their mother. And let Sarla Devi, the Chief of the Guild of the Great Goddess, accompany them so that all the rites may be properly observed.'

The crowd cheered. Jyanvi watched the platform from which the Matriarch had addressed the crowd on the Day of Oracles. There was some activity there, but Shyamila and Sarla had not appeared.

'What if they hold Gagri the Good and Sona as hostages?' Jyanvi blurted out.

The three Mayans looked at her, but did not answer. It was the sort of look that made Jyanvi shrink back.

'What was so bad about what I said?' she whispered to the Blue Donkey.

'From the Mayan point of view,' the Blue Donkey whispered back, 'I think you thought the unthinkable.'

There was movement on the platform now. Shyamila and Sarla Devi had presented themselves. Behind them were two other women accompanied by children. It was the expression on Saraswati's face that made Jyanvi realise that the child clinging to Malini Devi's hand was Sona and that the other child, who seemed to be trying to wrap herself in Pramila's sari, was Gagri the Good.

'Shall we haul them up?' Jyanvi enquired.

'No, we'll descend.'

'Yes, Your Majesty.' It seemed appropriate now to address her so.

The Matriarch smiled at Jyanvi kindly. 'You and the Blue Donkey must remain on board a little longer. Give the fleet the necessary orders to keep them occupied for a day or two. Then join us.'

Jyanvi and the Blue Donkey said they would do so. 'Your Majesty – ' the Blue Donkey hesitated. 'Will you be taking an escort with you?'

'An escort?'

'Well, a troop of Gallants.'

The Matriarch shook her head. 'No,' she said. 'I think this time we'll be all right. I'll take precautions.'

Asha the Apostate smiled reassuringly. 'We'll look after her, and soon you'll be with us.'

Shortly afterwards the three Mayans left the ship. As the Matriarch descended the Mayans cheered and shouted their welcome. They liked their Ranisaheb and thought that this aerial descent was worthy of her.

On the flagship the Blue Donkey turned to Jyanvi, 'How will you keep the Gallants amused?'

'It's easy,' Jyanvi replied. 'I shall encourage them to prance and strut.'

'What do you mean?'

But Jyanvi was already issuing orders to the Allied Chiefs to meet her on board in precisely an hour. The Blue Donkey busied herself with making sure that the supplies they carried were in good order. Jyanvi spent the next little while relaying the outline of her epic poem to the Slogan Writers. Then she brushed her uniform and smartened herself up. At the appointed time the Chiefs of the Allied Forces were welcomed aboard with military honours. They in turn saluted their Commander with proper deference.

'O Chiefs,' Jyanvi told them, 'the pleasure of the Mothers is the code in accordance with which we have lived our lives. Now the eyes of the Matriarch of Maya and of all the Mayan Mothers are upon us. For two days and nights can you put on a display of fire and water and aerial skills that does honour to them and is worthy of us?'

'Yes,' cried the Chiefs all in chorus. 'Yes, we can.'

'Then do so,' commanded Jyanvi, and dismissed them with an appropriate gesture.

For the next forty-eight hours the Gallants of Paradise put on a most spectacular show of waterworks and fireworks in the Mayan sky. The mothers of Maya were generous in their praise, as were Jyanvi and the Blue Donkey and the Mayan royalty, when affairs of state permitted them to look up.

20

Is that what you mean?

Perhaps nothing had changed, Jyanvi thought. Perhaps the exile and the wandering had only been a diversion. Shyamila the Civil had not been locked up. Sarla Devi, though no longer a Chief, was still at liberty to walk about. Valerie, of course, was still absent. When she had tried to warn the Mayans about the Trader Robots, they had refused to believe her. The tale was incredible. And so she had returned to Ashagad in the hope of somehow establishing their existence. The only other difference was Asha's presence – that and the fireworks in the sky. But otherwise it could have been any other evening. Dinner was over, and here they all were, sitting around. Any moment now Jyanvi expected the Matriarch to say, 'Amuse me.' But she was wrong. Within the next fifteen minutes Jyanvi realised that nothing was going to be the same any more.

The Matriarch was addressing Shyamila, 'Tell me, what is it you really want?'

Shyamila forced herself to meet her mother's eyes. 'Mother, why do you mock me?' She spoke with some impatience. 'I admit that I conspired against you. Punish me and be done.'

'Answer me.' The Matriarch was adamant. 'What do you want?'

'Very well,' Shyamila answered, 'if we must play this game. I want what I've always wanted. I want to rule.'

To everyone's astonishment the Matriarch smiled, 'Yes, you do, don't you? Well, you are appointed the Supreme Mother of the Armada of the Gallants. They're unruly children,' she added as an afterthought. 'Perhaps you can give them a sense of direction.'

'Me?' Shyamila was caught off balance. 'You want me to lead the Gallants? But what am I to do with them?'

'Rule them,' the Matriarch replied serenely. 'Sarla Devi will accompany you. The two of you must lead the Gallants on a voyage of discovery.'

Shyamila stared at the Matriarch in disbelief. 'But Mother, doesn't it occur to you that we could use the Armada against Maya Diip and thus gain power? Is this a trap?'

The Matriarch did not hide her weariness. 'Shyamila, the Gallants are children with toy balloons, capable of destruction, but to what purpose? You're a good administrator. I think you'll find the Gallants more challenging than the mothers of Maya. Go where you're needed. Help them to make something of themselves.'

There had been no unkindness in the Matriarch's voice. Wasn't her mother angry with her? Shyamila the Civil didn't know what to say. 'Yes, Mother,' she said at last.

The Matriarch then turned to Pramila the Poet. 'Will you go with your sister?'

Pramila blinked. 'As fellow administrator?'

'No, as Principal Poet.'

'What would be my duties?'

'Your principal duty,' the Matriarch told her, 'would be to glorify the Gallants and define their quest.'

'Well, yes.' But Pramila was uncertain. 'What about my responsibilities here on Maya?'

'You're relieved of them.'

The words startled Pramila. She tried to decide whether what had just happened was good or bad. She decided that it was bad. 'Mother,' she said quickly. 'I've changed my mind. I want to stay.'

'All right,' returned the Matriarch. 'Stay then.'

'What would you do if I asked to stay?' Shyamila asked suddenly.

The Matriarch looked at her. 'Do you want to stay?'

'No.'

'Then go with my blessings.'

Shyamila faltered for a moment. Could her mother dismiss her so easily? Then she stood up, walked over to her mother, touched her feet and left the room. Soon afterwards Pramila mumbled that she had a headache and made her excuses.

It was difficult to know what the Matriarch was thinking. Had Shyamila's departure made her sad? She looked tired, but her features were composed. Jyanvi watched her every movement. The Matriarch gave her attention to her remaining daughters and to Jyanvi and the Blue Donkey. They waited.

'It remains only to dispose of the Matriarchy of Maya,' she said.

They absorbed her words. Asha and Saraswati were too stunned to speak, but Jyanvi cried out. 'Why?' she begged. 'The Matriarchy of Maya is safe in your hands, and all is well.' Only the Blue Donkey showed no reaction.

The Ranisaheb was shaking her head. 'I've abdicated,' she told them calmly. 'Tomorrow I shall return to the forest.'

The words sank in. 'It's not yet time,' Saraswati protested. Asha said nothing. To have found her mother and to lose her so soon? She kept her grief to herself.

The Matriarch spoke gently, but her resolve was unshakeable. 'It's time.'

'But who's to be the next Matriarch?' Saraswati pleaded. It seemed to Jyanvi that Saraswati still hoped that her mother would take charge, and everything would work out in the end.

The Matriarch's reply disabused them. 'That's a matter that it's best you agree upon among yourselves. The three of you must decide with the Blue Donkey's help.'

She rose to her feet and the others stood up. The three women touched her feet as Shyamila had done. Then she embraced each one of them, including Jyanvi. Nobody wept. They were formal and seemly though they knew they were saying farewell. When she had gone, they looked at one another. They felt bereft. Outside the palace the sky was lit up by the fireworks of the Gallants. They turned to the Blue Donkey.

'Sleep on it,' the Blue Donkey advised them.

The next morning the sky was still crowded with the displays of the Gallants. The two Mayan princesses and Jyanvi faced the Blue Donkey in the rose garden. The three women were sitting on a bench. All in a row, almost like schoolgirls, the Blue Donkey thought.

'Well,' she began, 'which of you would like to be the Matriarch of Maya?'

It was Saraswati who spoke first. 'It's not so much for my own sake as for the sake of my daughter, Sona, that I feel it's right that I should be the next Matriarch.'

Asha the Apostate stared at her. 'What has any of this to do with your daughter? I also have a daughter, Gagri, whom I hardly know. But surely, even if you are the next Matriarch, it's been established for years that Gagri the Good will be your successor.'

Saraswati looked stubborn. 'That's not so.'

'Well then,' Asha the Apostate announced hastily, 'I claim the throne on behalf of my own daughter.'

'What about you?' the Blue Donkey looked at Jyanvi, but Jyanvi shook her head.

Saraswati was indignant. 'Aren't you going to support my claim?' she asked Jyanvi.

But Jyanvi seemed to be in a daze. 'What claim?' she mumbled.

'Don't you remember?' Saraswati was annoyed that Jyanvi and the Blue Donkey had to be reminded. 'On the Day of Oracles I was declared the true heir.

> "She who shall reign in the goddess' name
> must suffer change, yet stay the same." '

'But that describes me!' Asha exclaimed. 'I was exiled, not you.'

'At the time the Oracle was interpreted differently,' Saraswati replied coldly. 'And in any case, how can you reign? You committed heresy against Maya.'

'And you're such a true Mayan that you've lost the ability to think for yourself!' Asha retorted.

The Blue Donkey stopped the altercation. 'Since the two of you can't agree, shall we consider the third candidate?'

'The third candidate?' Asha and Saraswati both looked surprised. 'Are you in the running?' Saraswati enquired.

The Blue Donkey shook her head. 'No, I mean to join the Matriarch in the forest.'

'Do you mean Jyanvi?' Asha the Apostate asked suddenly. 'But you don't want to reign, do you?' Asha continued, addressing Jyanvi.

Jyanvi had been shaken by the news that the Blue Donkey was also leaving her. 'Don't leave me!' she wanted to cry out to the Matriarch and the Blue Donkey. 'Or take me with you into the forest. I'll look after you and find berries for you. I will be good.' She was close to tears. 'What?' she asked when she realised that Asha the Apostate had been speaking to her.

Asha repeated the question. 'Do you want to reign?'

'No,' Jyanvi replied. 'No, I never wanted to reign.'

Asha the Apostate looked at her intently. 'But would you if asked?'

'How can she make a good Matriarch if she doesn't even want to reign?' Saraswati interjected.

'Perhaps that's the best qualification,' Asha murmured. She looked straight at Jyanvi. 'Look, I must return to Ashagad. They need me there. But I must first look after Gagri's interests. Will you look after Gagri for me?'

Jyanvi evaded the question. She turned on the Blue Donkey. 'But why don't you and the Matriarch remain in Maya?'

'No,' replied the Blue Donkey. 'The Matriarch has gone and I must follow soon. Are you willing to take her place?'

'How can I?' returned Jyanvi. She stood up in exasperation

and glanced at Saraswati in the hope that Saraswati would back her up.

But Saraswati had become thoughtful. She spoke slowly, 'When I first knew you, there were many things you didn't know. I now realise that there are many things I don't know. If you choose to be Matriarch, you have my support.'

'But the oracle doesn't fit,' Jyanvi protested.

'Yes, it does. You've changed, haven't you?' Saraswati replied.

Jyanvi tried another tack. 'Don't you see,' she explained to the others, 'the mothers of Maya would never accept me. I'm not even a native Mayan, let alone a Mayan princess.'

'As Gagri's Guardian and my Consort, they would accept you,' Saraswati told her quietly.

'Will you look after Gagri the Good for me?' Asha repeated.

Jyanvi looked at them helplessly. 'I'm unfit,' she pleaded.

'Yes,' agreed the Blue Donkey equably. 'There's that.'

They waited for Jyanvi's reply in silence. In the sky overhead there was a sudden burst of noise and colour. Sarla Devi and Shyamila the Civil were ascending heavenward.

Jyanvi pointed to them. 'Is that what you mean?'

But Asha the Apostate replied steadily, 'No, that's not what we mean.'

Jyanvi turned to the Blue Donkey. Surely the Blue Donkey would come to her rescue? But the Blue Donkey seemed to be fading away as though already halfway to the forest. She put her arm on the Blue Donkey's neck. 'Why me?' she begged.

'By default.' The Blue Donkey's answer when it reached her ears was clear and dispassionate.

Jyanvi turned away ruefully. 'All right,' she said to her friends at last. 'Come on, then.'